for the

Love

of the

Baron

The Noble Hearts, Book 3

CALLIE HUTTON

Author's website: http://calliehutton.com/
Cover design by Erin Dameron-Hill
Manufactured in the United States of America

First Edition July 2018

ISBN 10: 1724634623
ISBN 13: 978-1724634627

ABOUT THE BOOK

Lady Marigold Smith, daughter of the Earl of Pomeroy and his last daughter to be married off, cannot find a man as intelligent as she is or who treats her like more than a featherheaded piece of fluff. So the spinster state is fine with her.

Jonathan, Lord Stanley, belongs to the same elite book club as Lady Marigold, who annoys him to no end. In his esteemed opinion, she is nothing more than a nonsensical chit who doesn't deserve membership in their exclusive club.

When they both attempt to buy the same journal of a deceased member, a man well-respected in the science community, a tug of war begins. The battle for the book throws them into danger—and passion. Something neither of them expected.

Thank you for choosing to read *For the Love of the Baron*.

I love my fans, and as a special treat,

I have something extra for you at the end of the story.

Enjoy!

DEDICATION

To Doug, husband, beta reader, and brainstorming partner.

CHAPTER ONE

April, 1822
London, England

Jonathan, The Right Honorable Lord Stanley, entered the bi-weekly meeting of the Gentlemen and Ladies Literary Society of London, handed his hat, cane and great coat to the man at the door, took two steps and cringed at the sound of Lady Marigold's laughter. Not that his fellow member laughed like a horse, or any other grating-on-the-nerves sound, but she was *always* laughing. Certainly, her life wasn't that funny. The chit didn't seem to take anything seriously.

'Twas probably why after more than a few Seasons, she remained a spinster. Truth be known, the girl didn't resemble any spinster he'd ever seen. Her curly dark blonde hair was always in disarray, but unlike other decorous maidens, that failing didn't appear to trouble her at all. Her hazel eyes, which he'd seen up close only one time when he'd danced with her at Everson's ball, had a sparkle to them that always put him on edge. As if she was planning something she knew he would disapprove of.

Yes, there were many things about Lady Marigold that set his teeth to grinding, and his skin to itching. As usual, she was surrounded by a bevy of men, a handful young, a few old, and several in between. She held them captive with some sort of story that he was sure was not anything worth listening to. Despite himself, he picked up a glass of warm lemonade and made his way to the group. Even if she was spouting a bit of nonsense, it might be a way to pass the time before the meeting began.

Why someone as flighty and silly as Lady Marigold belonged to this very proper book club baffled him every time he attended. Surely, she had better things to do with her time, like looking over fashion plates, selecting ribbons, and discussing the next ball with equally silly ladies.

He sipped slowly, not hearing anything coming from those plump lips, but watched the animation on her face as she spoke. Her generous breasts rose and fell as she took deep breaths and related her tale. She waved her hands in a most unladylike fashion as she spoke. Had the girl no training in proper decorum? Of course her mother had died when the chit was young, but someone should have taken her in hand by now.

"Don't you agree, Lord Stanley?" He started at her question when he hadn't been listening to anything but the grousing voice in his head. As if she suspected as much, she grinned at him with that smile that always annoyed him as well. Since most times it was directed at him in a way that made him feel like he'd just missed something important and was a dunce to have not noticed it. Blast the girl.

"I am sorry, my lady, but I am afraid I was woolgathering. Excuse me for being so impolite."

Lady Marigold opened her mouth to respond when Lord Dunkirk, president of the club, announced it was time for the meeting to begin. She flashed Jonathan a look that told him she knew he was happy to discontinue the banter she was surely prepared to engage in. And he would never come out the winner.

Once they all took their seats, Lord Dunkirk cleared his throat and addressed the audience. The speaker, who'd been the president for more than two years, sported a full beard and mustache, which Jonathan had long guessed hid scars from Dunkirk's time in His Majesty's service. From what Jonathan had heard, Dunkirk had served well, and bore the physical memory of his time there. He also used a sturdy cane to walk, again most likely from a war injury.

"Before we begin the discussion on our selected book of the week, Lord Byron's *The Vision of Judgment*, I would like to make an announcement."

He waved a cluster of papers fisted in his hand. "Our former member, Lord St. Clair, as you all know, passed several months ago. We are all sorry for the loss of his insight into the literary works we have discussed over the years. However, his nephew and heir, the new Lord St. Clair, is selling quite a bit of the former viscount's personal belongings."

Once again, he raised the papers. "In my hands, I have a list of what is to be offered at the estate sale on Saturday, next. I shall pass it around to the membership so each of you might examine the list.

There are numerous household items, but I am sure most of you will want to take special note of the books that are being offered for sale. St. Clair had quite a collection in his library."

He handed the notes to Lady Banburry, seated in the front row. Without even glancing at the documents, she passed them to Mr. Fiddle, sitting next to her.

Jonathan soon became engrossed in the discussion of *The Vision of Judgment*, and forgot about the papers until they arrived in his hands. Keeping one ear attuned to the discussion, he perused the list, flipping the pages as he went. On the fourth page, he stopped halfway down, his heart hammering in his chest.

Journal of Dr. Vincenzio Paglia (1800-1821).

Grasping the papers tightly in his hands, Jonathan blew out a breath and sat back in his chair. How the devil had St. Clair gotten ahold of the personal journal of the most famous man in Anatomy? His work and writings were renowned—at least in the circles Jonathan favored—and having the man's private journal, reading his thoughts and ideas, would be an absolute treasure to own. And one he had no intention of passing up.

With a smile on his face, he skimmed the rest of the sheets, nothing of major interest, but possibly a few tomes he might be inclined to purchase. However, no other item was near the consequence of the journal. He passed the papers along, and settled back to resume listening to the lecture, excited for the following Saturday to arrive.

***

Lady Marigold Smith, third and the last unmarried daughter of the Earl of Pomeroy, at the ancient age of two and twenty years, shifted in her seat as Mr. Boswick droned on and on about his understanding of the poem they were discussing.

Goodness, she hated when their assigned reading for the week was poetry. She loathed it and wanted to read more fiction. But since several members— especially that stiff-necked Lord Stanley—thought she wasn't serious enough to belong to the esteemed group, she would not give them the satisfaction of nodding their heads and looking at each other when she asked for the latest Anna Marie Porter or Jane Harvey book.

Oftentimes she questioned why she continued with the group. The answer was always the same. She did not like spending all her time on balls, routs, afternoon calls, and shopping. Or talking to the young ladies who enjoy that to the exclusion of everything else. Her secret love of Anatomy and Mathematics kept her distant from the other young ladies of the *ton*.

Yet, her vivacious and outgoing personality could not be hidden, and consequently, every time she attempted to be serious about something she was met with smiles, condescending looks, and complete dismissal of what she said. Too many times she felt like a small child being patted on the head because she had gotten her letters right.

And no one was as annoying as Lord Stanley. She had to admit the man was easy on the eyes. Tall, broad shouldered, deep chocolate brown eyes and wavy hair that continued to fall on his forehead. She couldn't imagine any part of him not obeying his command, so how his hair got away with it she didn't know.

But his comely face was held up by such a stiff neck it was a wonder the man could move his head from side to side. He always looked at her as if she had something nasty on her face. Of course, that only made her want to annoy him more. The one time he'd asked for a dance at Everson's ball, she tried her best to be pleasant to him, but he scowled at her the entire time. Why did he even ask for a dance if he disliked her so?

She shrugged her dismissal of the baron just as she was handed the papers on the estate sale being passed around for the members to view. She withdrew her spectacles from her reticule and slipped them on her face. Her vision had been poor since she'd been a child. It had never bothered her to wear them since her sisters and father saw nothing wrong.

However, once her finishing governess had arrived to train her sisters, Elise and Juliette, as well as Marigold, in the ways of the *ton*, and how to behave to catch a husband, the woman had told her in no uncertain terms that gentlemen do not approve of women who wore spectacles. That statement had thrown a young Marigold into a panic. She could not see very well without them, and here she was supposed to make her debut in a few years and stumble around the ballroom!

Her current chaperone and companion, Lady Crampton had dismissed the training governess's ideas and told Marigold she would be much more attractive to a gentleman if she wasn't walking into walls and plowing over potted plants.

She loved Lady Crampton.

Marigold ran her gloved finger down the list of the first couple pages. Nothing appealed to her, since Lord St. Clair had apparently been quite fond of hunting and husbandry as many of the books for sale were of that ilk.

She flipped to the fourth page and her finger stopped at a listing.

Journal of Dr. Vincenzio Paglia (1800-1821)

Dr. Paglia? The most notable figure in Anatomy? His discoveries of how the body functioned and was framed were held in a great deal of esteem by his colleagues. To think the daily recording of his days, activities, thoughts, and ideas, in his own handwriting, could be in her possession!

Two gentlemen sitting in front of her both turned and glared, making her realize she'd been talking out loud. Another trait of hers that annoyed those staid and pompous members of the club.

Too excited by far at the thought of obtaining the journal, she didn't allow their scowls to bother her. Smiling brightly, she turned the papers over to Miss Granger and tried once more to focus on Mr. Boswick's treatise which seemed to have no end.

Bright the following Saturday morning, Marigold pulled on her gloves and tapped her foot impatiently in the Pomeroy townhouse entrance hall as she waited for her father's carriage to be brought around.

"Are you sure you don't want me to go with you, Marigold?" Lady Crampton walked down the stairs, a shaft of papers in her hand. Most likely the following week's menu that she generally went over with Cook on Saturday afternoons.

"No, thank you for offering, but I will be fine by

myself. Now that I am labeled as 'on the shelf' I can enjoy the freedom I could not just a couple of years ago."

Lady Crampton stopped in front of Marigold and rested her palm on Marigold's cheek. "You are not 'on the shelf' my dear. You are a lovely young woman of only two and twenty years. Far from a spinster."

Marigold smiled back at the woman she'd known for only a few years but had grown as close to as a mother. "Perhaps not in your eyes, but certainly in the eyes of the *ton*."

Her chaperone smoothed back the hair that was forever falling out of Marigold's hairdo. "When the right gentleman comes along, he will no doubt sweep you off your feet and it will not matter how others view you."

Marigold reached in and kissed her on the cheek. "You have been reading too many fairy tales to your daughters."

The butler, Macon, opened the door and bowed. "Your carriage has arrived, my lady."

With excitement at her upcoming purchase, she hurried down the stairs and into the carriage.

CHAPTER TWO

Jonathan entered Lord St. Clair's small estate outside of London. He had arrived right on the dot of ten o'clock, the time stated in the paperwork as when the sale would begin.

He'd never met the nephew who was offering the items since St. Clair had been living on the continent and only returned once the former lord had passed. St. Clair had been forced to accept the title that gossips held was unwanted by the new viscount.

St. Clair stood apart from the would-be purchasers who browsed the room, picking up various items, and then putting them down again. The man was short of stature and on the plump side. If he was unhappy with the new title, it showed in his face. However, he had hired a man to handle the sale, who was quite busy dealing with the strollers, leaving St. Clair leaning against one wall, watching his man's every move. Perhaps he was afraid he would be cheated.

Jonathan wanted to ignore most of the items laid out for sale, and go straight for the journal, but he would most likely pay a steep price for it if it was known how much he wanted it. Better to find it, keep an eye on it, and then make his move after several minutes.

His eyes moved rapidly as he glanced from item to item until he gave out a deep breath and viewed the most coveted item he would ever own.

The Journal of Dr. Vincenzio Paglia (1800-1821)

There it was, right in front of him, in the renowned scientist and doctor's handwriting. It covered the last twenty-one years of the man's life. The time when he was working on a number of projects, some of which had been written up and hailed as genius, and some—Jonathan was sure— thoughts and ideas that had never come to fruition.

His hand trembled as he reached for the book then quickly snatched it back. Calm. He must be calm. Taking up a position not far from the journal, he pretended interest in other things to give himself a bit of time before claiming the tome.

"What a lovely home you have here, Lord St. Clair." *Bloody hell.* That voice. *She* was here. What the devil did Lady Marigold want with dusty old possessions of the dead Lord St. Clair?

He followed her movements from the corner of his eye. She chatted with other shoppers, laughed a great deal—of course—and picked up various things, then placed them back again.

His heart nearly came to an abrupt halt when she stopped in front of the journal and reached her hand out. Without even thinking, he dove in her direction and planted his hand on the journal just as she reached it, his hand holding the bottom of the book, her hand holding the top.

He tugged.

She tugged.

They both tugged.

Neither one released the book.

They glared at each other and tugged again.

Both held on tight.

"My dear Lady Marigold, I am afraid I was about to purchase this item."

Her raised eyebrows and the cool dismissive look on her face didn't affect him at all. He would not lose this book to this flighty, featherbrained woman. "Indeed? Then why was it laying on the table?"

He stiffened, not happy to justify himself to her. "I was about to pick it up."

They both tugged.

Neither one released the book.

"I believe as a lady, I hold precedence." Her lips moved into a smile that he'd seen over a card table right before he lost fifty pounds.

"No, my lady. I believe since I am a man, *I* hold precedence."

"You overestimate your consequence, my lord."

They both tugged.

Neither one released the book.

"Here, here. What is going on?" The man supervising the sale hurried over to them.

"Nothing at all is going on, my good man. I was about to purchase this item when this lady—he emphasized the word—took it out of my hand." Jonathan grinned, which he was afraid came out more like a grimace.

11

Lady Marigold gasped. "That is not true. I had it in my possession and he pulled it out of my very hand!"

They both tugged.

Neither one released the book.

The man plucked the journal out of both of their hands. "Good morning, my lady, my lord. I am Mr. Sedgewick, Lord St. Clair's man of business. May we please retire to the drawing room where we can discuss this out of the hearing of his lordship, who is having a bad day as it is?" He waved them forward. "It is difficult to sell off a love one's possessions."

From what Jonathan had heard, there had been not only no love lost between the new and prior Lord St. Clair, but barely any contact over the years.

They followed the man out the door, down the corridor and into another room, both glaring at each other.

The room was as dim and dull as the library where the sale was being conducted. Dust covers blanketed every piece of furniture in the room. The three of them all coughed at the amount of dust in the room.

Mr. Sedgewick ushered them to the French doors, which he pushed opened to allow fresh air inside. "I think perhaps it might do our lungs well to have our discussion out here."

Jonathan and Lady Marigold nodded and settled themselves on a couple of rickety chairs surrounding an equally rickety table. Mr. Sedgewick placed the journal on the table. Jonathan licked his lips. Lady Marigold sighed.

"From what I just witnessed, and your statements, I presume you both wish to purchase this journal."

***

Marigold leaned forward on her chair. It creaked enough she was afraid to continue to move, lest she end up on her bottom on the ground. Wouldn't His Stiffness, Lord Stanley love to witness that ignominious sight. Sitting very still, she offered the man a bright smile. "Yes, Mr. Sedgewick. I have a very strong reason to want to purchase that journal." She glared at Lord Stanley. "And I had it first."

"Her ladyship did not have it first. I arrived before her, as you must remember, Mr. Sedgewick, and had fully intended to purchase the book. In fact, it was in my hand when Lady Marigold grabbed it from me."

She jerked back. The chair creaked again, tilting to the side. She grabbed the edge of the table in front of them and held her breath, but the chair remained upright. "I did not grab it, Lord Stanley!"

Mr. Sedgewick raised his hands. "One moment, please." He looked back and forth between them. "Do you know each other?"

Marigold smoothed her gown, not looking up from her lap. "Yes. You might say so."

"And why is that?"

"Lady Marigold and I belong to the same literary society." Lord Stanley's mumbled words could hardly be heard.

Mr. Sedgewick grinned, as if he'd just solved a very delicate problem. "Well, then. This should be an easy matter to solve. I shall hold the journal with me, and I suggest you both go somewhere for tea and discuss the matter between you. I am sure you will come up with a solution that won't involve fisticuffs." He laughed at his own words, but neither Marigold nor Jonathan smiled.

She wanted that journal. There would be so much information in there about anatomy, that as a woman she had no access to. This would be her golden opportunity to further her studies without having to fight to gain access to such knowledge.

After an uncomfortable silence, Lord Stanley spoke up. "Yes, I believe that might be a good idea." His jaw was so tight it was a wonder it didn't break. "That is if Lady Marigold agrees, which I doubt."

Honestly, the man was extremely difficult to deal with. However, if she gave in to her desire to pop him over the head with her reticule, it would only prove his point. And possibly make Mr. Sedgewick think twice about allowing her to purchase the book.

She would take the adult stance and agree, just to prove him wrong. "Very well. I shall be thrilled to have tea with Lord Stanley and discuss the purchase of *my* journal." Marigold stood, and the two men jumped up. Mr. Sedgewick's chair tilted to one side, then slowly fell over, the wood on the arm splintering into a dozen pieces.

Mr. Sedgewick viewed the chair with raised brows. "I guess we shall not expect to receive significant remuneration from these household goods."

Marigold followed Mr. Sedgewick through the French doors, passed the dusty room, into the corridor, and to the front entrance. They passed the library where many more potential buyers had arrived while she and Stanley had battled over the journal.

The man of business came to a stop next to the butler at the door and turned to them. "I shall hold the journal for two hours, then I am afraid I must place it back on the table for sale." He bowed and pivoted on his heels, the sound of his footsteps echoing down the long corridor.

"I shall call for my carriage." Lord Stanley moved toward the butler.

"No."

He turned back, his brows raised. "Have you changed your mind, Lady Marigold? Shall I tell Mr. Sedgewick the journal is mine?"

"Absolutely not. I just don't agree we should travel in your carriage. I have my carriage with me as well, and I find it quite comfortable."

Lord Stanley moved close enough to her that Marigold could see the deepness of his brown eyes. She could also smell the scent of something citrus, and spicy. The heat radiating from his body made her uncomfortable. The surrounding air seemed to disappear, and she was having a hard time filling her lungs. Rattled, she eased back.

"Are you suggesting my carriage is uncomfortable?" Lord Stanley growled.

Marigold raised her chin. "I have no idea, since I have never ridden in it. However, I prefer my carriage."

Lord Stanley snatched his hat from the butler and jammed it on his head, bringing the brim almost to his eyebrows, likening to a child wearing his father's hat. "Very well, *Lady Marigold,* we shall ride in *your* carriage. Anything to bring this distasteful meeting to an end."

Marigold pulled on her gloves. "If you will have

my carriage brought around, sir, I would appreciate it." The butler, still holding his wooden stance, but with a slight twinkle in his eyes, nodded. "Very well, my lady. It will be just a minute."

He left them to summon the carriage while Marigold stood with her arms crossed, tapping her foot on the black and white tile. Oh, the man was impossible. Why would he assume they would travel in his carriage? Men always behaved in that manner. They expected to give orders, have them obeyed, and no one—especially a woman—should question them.

That was precisely why she needed Dr. Paglia's journal. She was not permitted to join any organizations that had anything at all to do with the human body. As a well-bred, gentle woman, she was supposed to swoon and reach for her vinaigrette when any part of the human body was mentioned.

Nonsense. Her curiosity and intelligence had gotten her into trouble more than once, and she would not pass up this opportunity to expand her mind. Lord Stanley could just suck lemons. This journal would be hers.

They continued to ignore each other until the butler returned. "Your carriage is ready, my lady."

"Thank you." Before Lord Stanley could attempt to take her arm, she moved ahead of him to make her way down the stairs. It had begun to rain since she'd entered the house, and the steps were slippery. Taking a chance, she stepped away from the door, her foot slid out from under her and, arms flailing, she fell backward.

Right into Lord Stanley's arms.

CHAPTER THREE

No one was more surprised than Jonathan when the sweet-smelling, lushly curved Lady Marigold ended up in his arms. When her foot flew out from under her, he automatically put his arms out and she landed there, with his one arm wrapped around her waist and the other hand cupping her generous breast.

"Unhand me!" She struggled to have him release her, but her feet continued to slide out from under her on the steps, so he held tighter to keep her from landing on her arse.

She slapped his arms with her reticule—bloody hell, what did she carry in that thing, anyway?—and wiggle, which was the absolute wrong thing for her to do given where his hands were. "Lady Marigold, stop. Settle yourself, or you will end up on your bottom."

"I would prefer to be anywhere except where I am. Unhand me, I say!"

Stupid, stubborn woman. He moved his hand up from her breast and cupped her shoulder. "All right, now straighten yourself out."

They had reached the bottom of the steps by then and she pulled away from him, shifting her gown, and glaring at him. "That was totally unnecessary, my lord."

Perhaps totally unnecessary, but his lower parts had responded to having her so close to him, which annoyed him to no end. The last thing he wanted was to be attracted to the harridan.

She adjusted her hat and smoothed her gown, and lifting her chin, took a footman's hand and stepped up into the carriage. If it weren't for the rain falling now in a steady drizzle, he would climb up and ride with the driver. Anything to avoid Lady Marigold.

Once they settled in, he tapped on the ceiling of the coach, and the driver snapped the ribbons and the horses trotted away from the St. Clair estate and toward the small village adjacent to it. "Do you have a preferable place to have tea, my lady?" He might as well ask her first because if he just picked a pub or inn she would most likely announce she had the perfect spot that she always frequented, leaving him again looking like a fool.

"No. I have never been to this village. Are you familiar with Sturbridge?"

He shook his head. "No. But I'm sure there is an acceptable place for a cup of tea."

"And discussion."

"Yes. And discussion." He rested his booted foot on his knee and stared out the window of the carriage, watching the water drip down the glass. Lady Marigold put him into knots. He might as well admit it, since he'd known her for the two years they'd belonged to the literary society, and he always left her presence rattled.

She was perhaps one of the prettiest young ladies of his acquaintance. When she smiled her perfect smile—never at him—the entire room lit up. He had tried dancing with her one time, but unable to think of anything to say to the very popular social butterfly, he merely kept silent, and they had parted ways without him speaking so much as one word.

He'd always wondered why someone with as much vivaciousness, looks and, from what he'd heard, an impressive dowry, was not married. She had to have had numerous offers throughout the years. If he was correct, this had to be her fifth Season, which would make her about two and twenty.

Not a great age, but certainly close to being considered a spinster soon. Well, for whatever reason she was not married, with no husband to control her, so he had to deal with her. She had always been a conundrum. Her flighty, silly, always-laughing ways marked her as a foolish miss in his mind. One to be easily dismissed. Yet, she contributed to the discussions at the literary society meetings in a thoughtful and intelligent way.

Who was the real Lady Marigold?

Why did he care?

Now they found themselves at odds over the journal. He couldn't for the life of him imagine why she would want such a thing. To a woman such as her, it would be dry, incomprehensible, and even scandalous. A young, unmarried, gently reared woman had no interest in body parts, which he was sure the journal was filled with.

Dr. Paglia had made tremendous advancements in the study of the human body. Jonathan had been fascinated with the study of anatomy since he attended university. As a baron, it would not suit for him to practice medicine, but he certainly enjoyed keeping up on the latest discoveries. He read with a great deal of enthusiasm the monthly Journal of the Royal Society of Medicine.

The carriage came to a rolling stop at the east end of the village. The coach shifted as the driver dropped to the ground and opened the door. "Which shop will you be visiting, my lord?"

"Neither the lady nor I are familiar with the town, so perhaps you can question a shop or two and we will go with that."

"Very good." The man tugged on the brim of his hat, closed the door and walked off.

"I will be happy to compensate you in any way you deem acceptable if you renege on your request to purchase Dr. Paglia's journal." It might be worth the chance to attempt to assuage Lady Marigold's stubbornness with the book. Perhaps she really didn't want it but was merely being difficult by continuing to insist on owning it.

"I am afraid there is no compensation great enough for me to pass up the opportunity to own Dr. Paglia's journal, my lord."

Jonathan shifted in his seat, trying to keep his temper down, since yelling wasn't going to get him anywhere with the onerous woman. "Why in heaven's name would a woman like you want Dr. Paglia's journal?"

***

"A woman like me! What exactly do you mean by

that, Lord Stanley?" Her entire body tensed, and she quickly understood the long-held statement 'seeing red.' However, the red she saw was when she imagined pompous Lord Stanley lying in a pool of blood on the floor. With her holding the saber with which she'd run him through.

Lord, the man had the power to turn her into a bedlamite and led her to imagining things so very unlike her. She was a cheerful person by nature, liked most people, had dozens of friends, both male and female. For some reason she could not be in this man's company without wanting to wreak violence upon his person.

He actually stammered. "I apologize. I did not mean any disrespect. I merely am curious as to why a young, beautiful, charming young lady of the *ton* wishes to own a book written by a doctor about things that most young ladies would shy away from."

Before she could answer, the driver opened the door. "My lady it appears there is a small tea house two shops down, across the street."

"Thank you, John." She shifted to leave the carriage. "Just wait here for us. This won't take long." She accepted the driver's hand and climbed down, shaking out her skirts. Lord Stanley followed, and they walked across the street. Perhaps she was being stubborn after the disaster on the steps leaving St. Clair's house, but she would not accept Lord Stanley's arm.

It never paid to get too comfortable with the enemy.

For such a modest town, the tea house was delightful. The dark paneled walls held sconces that lit up the area, giving it a very warm and welcoming feel.

Several small tables were scattered around the room, with fresh linens and sparkling silverware on each.

She and Lord Stanley took a seat at table closest to the window that allowed the rare, but bright sunlight to swath their table with warmth and light.

"May I assist you, my lady, my lord?" A woman dressed in a starched black gown, covered by a pristine white apron approached them, a bright smile on her face. "May I recommend our scones? Cook makes the best in all of England."

Marigold couldn't help but smile at the woman. "I will definitely try some of the scones. They sound wonderful."

The woman dipped, then turned to Lord Stanley. "The same for you, my lord? Or would you prefer sandwiches?"

He waved the woman off. "Tea and scones is fine for me, as well. Thank you."

Marigold commented on their surroundings, making small talk until the tea and scones arrived. The woman arranged them all precisely on the table, poured two cups of the dark liquid into two dainty china cups and left them. Marigold added one lump of sugar and a dash of milk to her tea while Lord Stanley fixed his to his liking.

She took one sip, then set the cup down and faced him, forgetting for the moment the wonderful aroma coming from the scones. "I have as much right to own the journal of Dr. Paglia as you do."

Lord Arrogance raised his brows. "And why is that, my lady? No one has the 'right' to own a book that is for sale. One may merely offer to purchase it, pay the asked for price, and then it is given into their hands. Nothing 'rightful' about it." He popped a piece of scone into his mouth and smirked.

Oh, to wipe that look off his face with the clotted cream sitting in the bowl right next to her plate. However, wishing to conduct herself as a lady, she said, "Why is it you are so interested in the journal? Perhaps my reason is stronger than yours."

Lord Stanley leaned back in his chair and crossed his arms over his chest. "I have a great deal of interest in anatomy. I have studied it for years, and Dr. Paglia is the most renown man of this century in that field. The daily recordings of his thoughts and ideas would be fascinating to an aficionado of the genre."

Marigold leaned forward, Lord Stanley's words exciting her all over again. "I agree. It would be astounding to know what he thought of the things he later created, or things that never did make it past his drawing table. I have my own thoughts on what he imagined would be available in the world of medicine of the future."

His lordship's jaw dropped. "You know of Dr. Paglia?"

She leaned back and stared at him. "Of course, I do. Why do you think I want his journal?"

"I have no idea. I guess I assumed you wanted it for some silly female reason."

Her eyes narrowed, and the bowl of clotted cream was looking better as a decoration for Lord Arrogant's face. "Some silly female reason? Like what? Do you think I imagined his journal was full of writings on ribbon colors and ladies fashion?" She slammed her napkin down on the table and stood. "I can see where this entire conversation will lead us nowhere. You have absolutely no respect for me, or probably for any woman."

He jumped to his feet and held out his hands in a pleading fashion. "Please take your seat. I withdraw any comment I made that casts an unflattering light upon you." He waved at her seat. "Please?"

She reluctantly returned to the chair and placed her napkin on her lap again. "If we are to have a true compromise, we must refrain from suppositions and assumptions. Let me make this clear. I want the journal, for my own reasons, and you want it for your own reasons. That is the only thing that needs be discussed."

She leaned her elbow on the table, right in the bowl of clotted cream, and winced. "So, who gets the book, Lord Stanley?"

CHAPTER FOUR

Jonathan tried very hard not to laugh as he handed Lady Marigold his napkin to wipe her elbow. With her nose in the air, as if dipping her elbow into a bowl of clotted cream had been precisely what she had intended to do, she accepted the cloth and cleaned herself up. He had enjoyed watching the various emotions play over her face the entire time they'd been at the inn.

He didn't believe for one minute she was interested in anatomy and tried as hard as he could to figure out what her motivation was for wanting the book. She was a study in contradictions and didn't fit anywhere into his well-ordered life, and the way he placed most people he knew into well-defined boxes.

Lady Marigold was a definition of her own. Pretty, sharp-witted, shapely, intelligent, flighty, sensuous, yet something about her made him think what she showed the world was not the true Marigold. A man could spend a lifetime trying to unwrap all the layers of the woman.

On the other hand, he wished her to perdition, so he could get on with the purchase of Dr. Paglia's journal and retire to his comfortable library with a glass of brandy and the book. "Since Mr. Sedgewick gave us only two hours and then he intends to place the journal back up for sale, I suggest we get on with a solution or we will both lose it."

"I do not intend to give up. Do you, Lord Stanley?"

"No."

"Then I suggest we return to Lord St. Clair's estate sale and ask Mr. Sedgewick to decide who is to get the book."

Jonathan shrugged. "That would be an easy answer for him. He would most certainly sell it to the highest bidder."

"I possess a fortune, Lord Stanley, as I am sure you—and every other gentleman in the ton knows— and I intend to pay whatever I need to pay to possess the book."

Lord Stanley placed coins on the table and took her elbow to escort her out of the building. Remarkably enough, she did not pull back, but allowed him his gentlemanly manners. "Then I guess we must have Mr. Sedgewick decide the owner, then. I, too, possess enough coin to pay whatever is necessary to own the journal."

Lips tightened, they climbed into the carriage and headed back to the estate. The silence on the return ride was painful. He could not lose that book. He would happily spend the remaining evenings of his life going over and over the pages, delving into the mind and writings of the most remarkable man of the century. No, he would not give up.

There were about the same amount of interested parties browsing the library when they returned. Mr. Sedgewick was again going from patron to patron and speaking briefly with them, most likely negotiating prices.

Lord. St. Clair had not moved from his spot and still glared at everyone in the room as if an unidentified person was about to abscond with an article without paying for it. He was certainly a surly looking man.

Jonathan needed to get this over with. His fingers actually itched to touch the book again. He and Lady Marigold moved across the room and caught Sedgewick's attention. He raised his eyebrows as he approached them. "Do we have a solution, then? If not, I will have to insist on returning the book to the table for others to bid on."

Lady Marigold offered one of those smiles that most likely brought many a London gentleman to his knees. "I am afraid we are at a stalemate, Mr. Sedgewick. Perhaps we can impose upon you to decide who shall get the book?"

Bloody hell, the woman actually batted her eyelashes. Was there no pride whatsoever in the chit? One minute she was a serious contender for a book most women would not even care to touch, and then used her female wiles on the man.

"Ah, still unable to settle your differences?" Sedgewick tapped his chin and thought for a moment. "I believe the best solution is to ask the owner who he prefers to have the book."

Three pairs of eyes slid in Lord St. Clair's direction, who hadn't changed positions since the crowds had entered. This was probably the stupidest answer Sedgewick could have given them, but before Jonathan could object, the man strode over to where his lordship held up the wall, waving at Jonathan and Marigold to follow him.

"My lord, may I ask a question of you?" Sedgewick's voice was lowered to keep the others from hearing their discussion.

The man didn't answer, but only looked at his man of business.

Sedgewick continued, apparently undisturbed by the lack of response from St. Clair. "My lord, these two people both want to purchase this journal. They cannot decide between them who shall have it. I ask you to decide who you will sell it to."

"What is it?" He may have asked the question, but his dead eyes showed no real interest.

Sedgewick looked at the cover. "It appears to be the journal of a Dr. Paglia."

"Who is he?"

"I don't know." Sedgewick turned to Jonathan. "Who is this man?"

"Dr. Vincenzio Paglia is perhaps the most renown scientist and man of medicine of this century."

"The century is only two and twenty years," Lord St. Clair pointed out.

Would he never rid himself of dealing with morons? "Nevertheless, I am certain the book contains a great deal of information that someone like myself who is interested in anatomy would love to read, and own."

St. Clair waved at Mr. Sedgewick. "Give it to him."

Lady Marigold gasped. "But, my lord, I haven't

spoken, and I want the book, too."

St. Clair stared at her for a few minutes, his eyes roving over her body from the tips of her toes to the top of her head. "A woman has no need of such things. If you wish to know about anatomy, I will be more than happy to instruct you."

***

The next afternoon, Marigold lay sprawled on the settee in her drawing room with the book she was pretending to read laying open on her stomach and sighed once again.

Damn that Lord Stanley.

She was barefoot, and the large toe on her left foot peeked out from the hole her maid had fixed, but no longer held. Her hair was in disarray, and her skirts were around her knees. But she didn't care. All she cared about was losing that journal to Stanley.

The only saving grace for the man had been when he'd punched that obnoxious Lord St. Clair in the nose. Right after he'd given Mr. Sedgwick the amount of money he wanted for the journal and had the book in his hands. His lordship went down like a boulder dropped from a cliff.

Lord Stanley had glared at the man as he lay on the ground unconscious. "That was for insulting the lady."

He then cupped Marigold's elbow and practically pulled her from the house as she kept twisting and turning to see if Lord St. Clair was all right. Mr. Sedgewick was much too busy trying to revive his employer to worry about her and Stanley.

She clasped her hands over the flattened book

and sighed again, staring at the symmetrical pattern on the ceiling, trying to multiply the parts by the area to come up with…she didn't know. Despite her uncanny ability with numbers that had stunned Papa since she'd been a little girl, sometimes math failed her.

No more than two minutes later the sound of very loud—male—voices caught her attention. Before she could even sit up, Lord Stanley burst into the drawing room with her butler, Macon, right behind him. "I'm so sorry my lady, but the gentleman would not wait for me to announce him."

Lord Stanley came to an abrupt halt at the sight of Marigold. Spurred into action, she scrambled to a sitting position and smoothed her skirts, tucking her bare feet under her gown. "My lord. Do what do we owe the pleasure of this visit?"

Wasn't that what was said when a gentleman called on a young lady? It had been so long since she had encouraged anyone enough to do it, she'd forgotten.

His lordship marched right up to her and leaned over far enough that Marigold was practically climbing over the top of the sofa. "Where is it?" he growled. His warm breath scented with mint and something sweet wafted over her.

"Where is what?"

"Don't play false with me, Lady Marigold. Where is the journal?"

"I have no idea what you are talking about." They were face to face, almost nose to nose and her back was hurting. "Please move back, my lord. I am in pain."

He jerked himself up and paced, running his

fingers through his hair. "I knew you wanted that journal—for what reason I am still puzzled—but I never thought you would stoop so low as to steal it."

Marigold hopped up, landing on her twisted foot, losing her balance. Lord Stanley reached out and grabbed her and she fell against his body. Again. His rock-hard body. His well-scented, very warm body. She came to a complete standstill and stared up at him, licking her lips. His eyes were wide, and he looked at her like no one had ever looked at her before.

Especially a man.

He shook his head as if coming out of a trance. "The journal is missing, and I know you had something to do with it. If you didn't steal it directly, you had someone do it for you."

She pulled back and patted the back of her hair. Which didn't matter since it was all falling over her shoulders anyway. Lord, she must look a fright. "How dare you accuse me of thievery. I demand you leave my house immediately!"

He crossed his arms over his chest. "Not until I retrieve my journal."

"Well then you will have to go somewhere else because your journal—that *you* stole from *me*, I might add—is not here."

He raised his finger in the air. "Ah ha! You just admitted that you believe I stole the book from you, so now you feel it is your right to steal it back."

Marigold stomped her foot, which didn't offer too much of an impression since she was barefoot. "I did not steal your book." Once again, she pointed to the door. "Do I have to get one of the footmen to throw you out?"

"Children, children, whatever is going on in here?" Lady Crampton swept into the room, looking back and forth between Marigold and Lord Stanley.

After a few breaths, Lady Crampton pointed to the sofa. "Marigold, sit down." She turned to Lord Stanley. "Lord Stanley, I believe? Please take a seat. You two are so loud I heard you all the way upstairs in my bedchamber."

They both sat and glared at each other. Lady Crampton very delicately took a seat next to Marigold on the edge of the sofa, her back ramrod straight, just as she had tried numerous times to teach Marigold to do. Without success. "Have you rung for tea?"

They both stared at her companion. "Tea?" Marigold sputtered. "This man came here to accuse me of thievery."

Lady Crampton patted her hand. "Now, my dear, we will get to the bottom of this, but things always go better with tea." She turned to Lord Stanley. "Isn't that right, my lord?"

He looked as confused as Marigold felt. They had been in the middle of a blustering battle and Lady Crampton wanted to send for tea?

"Very well. I will send for tea." Marigold stood and stomped over to the brocade bell pull. "Perhaps with any luck his lordship will choke on it."

"Marigold. Really!"

CHAPTER FIVE

Jonathan reached the bottom step of the staircase to the Wycliffs' ballroom. Without even trying, he spotted Lady Marigold across the room. She was a woman he had pretty much ignored at social events for a few years and now his eyes zeroed in on her like an arrow for its mark.

He snorted. As usual, she was surrounded by numerous gentlemen. All ages, all shapes and sizes, and all clamoring for her attention. Since his recent encounter with the woman, he'd asked around at his clubs and it seemed Lady Marigold had a reputation.

Not a scandalous reputation, but nevertheless, it was known in Polite Society that she had broken a few hearts and turned down numerous men who had offered for her over the last four and a half years. Yet, they continued to flock to her side, begging for dances and the chance to eat supper with her.

Well, he wouldn't be one of those ninnyhammers who danced attendance on the chit. However, it was in his best interests to request a dance from the girl.

There was important information he needed to relate to her he'd only learned this morning, and he was anxious to speak with her.

The best dance, of course, would be a waltz since they would have the opportunity to speak freely. Also, a supper waltz would be preferable, so they could continue their conversation over their meal.

Striding with confidence across the room, he approached Lady Marigold just as Lord Hemmingway was leaving her group, most likely to find his partner for the upcoming cotillion. Before the man who had this dance with her could arrive, Jonathan slipped in and bowed to Lady Marigold. "My lady. You are looking exceptionally well this evening."

She viewed him with narrowed eyes. "Good evening, my lord."

"May I request the pleasure of standing up with you?"

Glancing down at the small card dangling from her wrist, she said, "I don't believe I have any dances left."

"Let me see." He ignored her shocked gasp as he took hold of her wrist and examined the card. She had been correct. There wasn't a single dance left. He quickly scanned the names and then bowed to her. "I am sorry to not have arrived sooner. Have a pleasant evening." He turned on his heel and began his search for Mr. Bridgewater. The man who had written his name on the line for the supper waltz.

While he searched for the man, he thought back to his visit two days ago to Marigold's townhouse. In retrospect, his behavior had been more storming the walls of the castle than a gentleman calling on a lady. He'd been absolutely certain Lady Marigold had either stolen the journal or arranged for it to be stolen.

Perhaps he should have treated the situation with a bit more finesse, but his anger had overtaken him when he retired to his library after a restful night's sleep, a hardy breakfast and practically rubbing his hands together to get to the journal.

That was when he found the book missing. After a brief, albeit fruitless search, he left the house, certain he would find the woman reading the journal when he arrived.

It had taken the tea Lady Crampton had suggested, along with an hour of conversation before he was convinced Lady Marigold had nothing to do with the journal missing. It was then, with his tail between his legs, he'd returned home and did some investigation.

What he'd discovered, combined with what he'd heard just this morning was, to say the least, disturbing. And like it or not, he wanted to bring Lady Marigold into the mix. He had grudgingly admitted the woman did know her anatomy, had mentioned she was gifted in math, and as he had suspected for some time, what the frivolous-appearing lady showed the world was not all there was to be seen.

That discovery, along with his body's annoying reaction to her nearness could possibly be the most disturbing factor in this entire matter. He'd always known he needed to marry one day and produce an heir or two. Always in his mind had been the image of a sweet, biddable, eager to please young girl.

He would train her in the running of his household to his liking, introduce her to the pleasures of the marriage bed—hoping she would not find the act too disagreeable, since he believed in fidelity—and have a happy, calm life.

That continued to be his aim, but he'd never thought he would be attracted to the flirty, silly, social butterfly who had now revealed herself as quite intelligent. She would never be biddable, would most likely run rampant over him and his staff, cause numerous issues that he would have to resolve, and never offer him the life he'd envisioned.

On the other hand, all that fire and enthusiasm would make bedsport quite a bit entertaining. To say the least.

An hour later, he arrived at Lady Marigold's side. "My lady, my dance, I believe."

She whirled from where she spoke with Lady Crampton. "What?" She checked her wrist. "Mr. Bridgewater has this dance."

He shook his head, arranging his features to show sadness. "I am sorry, my lady, but Mr. Bridgewater was called back home a bit of time ago. It seems one of his prize horses escaped the mews, and he was most anxious to find the animal."

Lady Marigold crossed her arms and narrowed her eyes. "And how is it you obtained this information?"

Jonathan shrugged, pretending indifference. "Because I was the one that brought the disturbing information to Mr. Bridgewater."

"How did you know this?"

"Um. I didn't really know this, but I assumed if one of his prized horses *did* escape the mews he would want to return home immediately."

Instead of the scowl and dismissal he'd expected, Lady Marigold laughed and shook her head.

And the sound of her laughter did not annoy him

at all.

***

Marigold extended her hand. "Very well, Lord Stanley. I will be honored to stand up with you." She had to give the man credit. For whatever reason, he'd wanted a dance with her, and made sure he got what he'd wanted. That was another point in his favor. She'd always viewed him as stiff-necked and condescending, with a way of looking down at people—especially her. The man she'd assumed he was, would not have pulled the trick he did tonight to get his way.

A disturbing thought, that.

He led her to the dance floor and placed his large, warm hand on her lower back. She shifted, suddenly aware of his scent, strength, and size. She took his hand and looked up into his eyes, and immediately looked away. This was not good. She must remember Lord Stanley was the enemy. He disapproved of her, accused her of thievery and most likely only wanted to dance to further question her.

She stiffened her shoulders and the music began.

After they gained their rhythm, he pulled her a little closer than she would have liked and bent his head. "There is important information I want to relate to you. That is why I maneuvered to gain this particular dance. We will have time to discuss it now, and then at supper."

Goose flesh broke out on her arms at his change in demeanor. "What is it?"

"I no longer believe you took my journal."

"That is all? All this trickery to merely tell me

what I've already told you?" Honestly, the man was so difficult to deal with. Here she'd thought they'd put the entire matter of her stealing his journal behind them. In fact, she had intended to request to borrow the book once he found where he had misplaced it. She was sure it hadn't been stolen, only his imagination had run away with him.

"No, listen. This morning I came across information that cast the missing journal into a whole new light."

"What is that?"

"Lord St. Clair is dead."

Marigold sucked in a breath and stumbled. Lord Stanley's strong arms kept her from falling to the ground. "Dead? He was a young man. He seemed in fine health when we saw him only a couple of days ago."

"Exactly. I find the entire thing questionable."

She frowned. "I don't understand."

He twirled them out of the way of another couple who were moving much slower. "First, I buy the journal and that very night—or morning—it is stolen. There is no doubt about that. My staff and I have torn the house apart. The journal is not there. Then the man who sold it to me ends up dead."

"You think they are connected?"

Lord Stanley shrugged. "Let's just say I have a large problem with coincidences." Once they reached the open French doors, he dipped and turned, and maneuvered them outside to the patio.

"Nice move, my lord." Marigold grinned. He grinned back, and something strange and interesting fluttered in her stomach. She was not used to his non-stuffy side. That new side was a view she could get into a great deal of trouble with.

As much as her opinion of the man was changing, she still didn't want to encourage him—or herself—in any romantic way because Lord Stanley would just not suit. She'd turned down numerous of offers over the years, but never had she second-guessed herself. Most men of the ton, and certainly the ones who courted her, opined that women had their place.

At afternoon calls, visiting modistes, selecting ribbons, gossiping, and managing their lord's households. That was not her intention for the rest of her life. She loved her interest in anatomy and did not want to push it aside to plump up some lord's imagined consequence.

Instead of taking her arm, he intertwined their fingers together and tugged her down the steps into the garden. They strolled a safe distance away to keep from being overheard, but close enough to the doors of the ballroom that scandal should not touch them.

Marigold looked back at the French doors and chewed her lip. "I should tell Lady Crampton where I am."

"We shall only be a moment. I want to tell you my theory and see what you think of it."

"You are soliciting my opinion? A mere woman? Good heavens, Lord Stanley, I am very impressed."

To her great surprise, he reached out and touched her lightly on her cheek, drawing his finger down to her jaw. Her lungs seized, and she had the absurd desire to lean in and touch her lips to his.

"Yes. I am seeking your opinion. It has come to my attention that you are not all fluff and nonsense, Lady Marigold. The question remains, why do you present yourself so?"

Because his voice rose on the last word of his statement, she assumed he'd asked her a question, but for the life of her she could not conjure up his words. He moved closer until their bodies were almost touching. "Why do you hide your intelligence?"

Oh, that was what he had asked her. Right now, any intelligence she possessed had vanished. "I'm not sure."

He grinned, as if he knew the effect he as having on her. Instead of leaning in farther to give her the kiss she hoped for, he pulled back and continued to walk. "My theory is St. Clair was killed for the journal."

Luckily, with them continuing the stroll, she had gained back some of her senses. "What do the police think?"

He hesitated. "They say his death was an accident."

Marigold studied him for a moment. "But you think otherwise."

"Yes. As I said, I am not a huge fan of coincidences."

He turned them so they were walking back to the patio. "What do you think?"

Marigold sighed. "Your theory makes a great deal of sense. But there is only one way to lay the matter to rest. In my mind, at least. I believe we need to view St. Clair's body."

Lord Stanley came to an abrupt halt. "What?"

She regarded him with her most innocuous expression. "View the body. See what it is that makes the police believe it was an accident when we think it was not."

"So you think it wasn't an accident as well?"

"I do. But my mind says we must be sure. If we learn St. Clair was murdered—and most likely for the journal—then there is something of great value in the book. And, the book is by rights, yours."

He gave her a curt nod as they continued up the steps from the garden to the patio. "Fine. In that case, I will go to the morgue later tonight to do my research. I understand they are holding him there while they trace another family member."

She shook her head. "No."

"Did you not just say the body needs to be viewed?"

"I did. But *you* are not going to the morgue. *We* are going to the morgue."

CHAPTER SIX

"I really don't think this is a good idea." Jonathan hurried Lady Marigold from the back door of her townhouse to where his carriage stood a block away. "It would make much more sense if I did this alone. I mean, a gently-bred woman breaking into the morgue in the middle of the night? I must have been addlepated to consent to this."

"If it eases your conscience any, my lord, I did not give you much of a choice. I insisted upon coming."

"Yes, but I am the idiot who agreed to it and am now absconding with you in the dark of night. If we are seen by anyone in the *ton*, your reputation is ruined."

Lady Marigold waved her hand in dismissal. "Nonsense. It was my decision, and I very much doubt if my reputation would be ruined. I am practically on the shelf now, anyway. No one wants a bluestocking spinster."

He couldn't understand Lady Marigold's

disparagement of herself. Did she not see all the men who flocked to her at every ball? Who lined up, practically licking their lips, to have the chance to hold her in their arms and dance? Foolish woman. She had no idea of her appeal.

They settled into the carriage, and Lady Marigold pulled her pelisse closer to her body, shivering.

"Here, come sit on this side, and I will keep you warm. There was a blanket under the seat, but my housekeeper took it to have it cleaned, and hasn't yet returned it."

"I get a bit nauseous when I sit with my back to the horses. Can you move over here?"

Jonathan switched seats and wrapped his arm around Lady Marigold's shoulders, pulling her close. She continued to shake, and he wasn't sure if it was from the cool, damp night, or her nerves. "Are you certain you want to do this? You can wait in the carriage and I can conduct the examination by myself."

"No. I have never had the opportunity to see a dead body."

"Thank God."

She turned her head to regard him. "This would do quite a bit for my studies in anatomy."

Her lips were close. Much too close. All he had to do was bend about two inches and they would kiss. Something he'd recently been considering far too much. The walk in the garden when they'd decided on this crazy adventure had left him frustrated and uncomfortable. Again, her flowery scent drifted from the warmth of their bodies pressed together. He had to get this situation cleared up so he didn't have to continue to be in her company. She was a distraction to his normally clear thinking, and kept him up nights remembering her laughter, her blonde curls, hazel eyes, and womanly curves.

She would never be the woman for him, so he had to stop these constant visions of Lady Marigold sprawled on his bed, naked as the day she was born, her golden hair spread over his pillows. He shifted in his seat.

In the interest of keeping his attention on what they were about to do, he pulled back and patted her hand. "I would like to one day talk to you about anatomy. I have made some discoveries myself and it amazes me how much new information about the human body is uncovered each year."

"Especially with the monthly Journal of the Royal Society of Medicine. There is always new and exciting information there."

Jonathan reared back. "How do you manage to read that magazine? It's only for men."

She smiled in a way that wanted him to forget about the magazine, forget about the morgue and take her someplace quiet, dark and secluded.

"I ordered a subscription in my papa's name. When it comes, Macon, our man at the door, knows to give it to me." She looked like the cat who stole the cream.

"Very clever, but I'm beginning to think you are a lot cleverer than you let on."

"So you've said." She moved her head and edged the curtain aside. "I believe we have arrived."

Ensuing quiet, almost a somber mood descended on them. The driver opened the door and let down the steps. Jonathan climbed out first and turned to help Lady Marigold down. "Are you sure you don't want to wait in the carriage? It will not diminish my respect for you in any way."

Lady Marigold shook her head. "No. This is something I will never have a chance to do again. I shan't let the opportunity pass me by."

The woman said the strangest things. "I should hope you never have the opportunity to view a dead body again. 'Tis not a pretty sight."

Lady Marigold took a deep breath. "Nevertheless, I am ready."

He reached out and again took her hand rather than placing it on his arm. For some reason, holding her thus anchored him, made him feel that whatever they were going to see they would handle together, and possibly clear up the mystery of the journal.

They went around the back of the building. Jonathan had done surveillance earlier in the day, thankfully under cover of drizzle and dark clouds. With everyone hurrying along, heads down, or umbrellas up, no one had paid him any attention. He had found a window, pushed it open just slightly, and placed a branch there to keep it open.

Jonathan had to feel his way along the bricks until he reached the window. He breathed a sigh of relief. It was still open. Without a word to Lady Marigold, he pulled the stick out and pushed up the window. He waited for a moment to listen for any sounds of someone checking the room.

Nothing. Except the heavy breaths coming from him and his partner in crime.

He waved to Marigold and leaned in close. "Stay here," he whispered. "I will climb in the window and pull you in after me."

She nodded, and he placed his hands on the

window sill and pulled himself up, landing in the dark room with a thud.

***

Marigold cupped her hands together and blew into them. Despite her gloves, her fingers were ice cold. Perhaps it wasn't just the weather, but the idea that she was about to view a dead body. A body she and Lord Stanley believed had been murdered.

Stanley stuck his head out the window. "Here, take my hands."

Marigold reached up and grasped his hands, and he began to pull her up. "Place your feet against the bricks, or you might get scraped as I pull you up. Sort of like you were walking up the wall." Even though his voice was low and soft she felt as though he was shouting.

She did as he said and within minutes she was inside the building, standing alongside him in the darkest room she'd even seen. She moved closed to his side.

"Are you well?"

"Yes." She wrapped her hands around her body and shivered. "It's just that I don't exactly care for dark places. Or small spaces."

"Let's get this over with." He took her hand and they walked across the room, wincing when they hit a squeaking board. "I asked for the layout of the building from a friend who had been here before to identify his brother's body when he drowned." Lord Stanley shivered. "The room where the bodies are kept is in the basement. They did not do an autopsy on St. Clair because the police said he tripped over something while intoxicated and hit his head against the brick on his fireplace."

He opened the door, and after looking side to side, pulled her out and they continued down the corridor to a very narrow staircase. Marigold held back when Lord Stanley started down the steps. He looked back at her with raised brows.

"It's so dark. And so narrow." Sweat beaded on her forehead and she wiped her damp palms against her skirts.

"I can return you to the carriage."

"No." She shook her head. "I will be all right."

He eyed her with concern, took one step down, then came back up to where she stood and wrapped his arm around her waist. "Tuck your head into my shoulder, and I'll lead us both down."

Feeling rather peculiar, but grateful for his understanding of this weakness without laughing at her, they began their descent. The closer they grew to the basement, the stronger the odor that assailed them.

"Oh, my, that is some very strong smell." The scent was so strong, her eyes were watering.

"Dead bodies do have an aroma about them. Place your hand over your face and breath through your mouth."

The basement was everything from her worst nightmares. Dark and damp with water dripping from the windows and down the walls from the rain outside. Jars with strange looking items in liquids were lined up on shelves along the walls. Two bodies lay on tables, with sheets covering them. Based on the bumps on the chest of one body, that one was a woman, which left the other body St. Clair.

"Suppose no one steps up the claim him? He can't continue to lay here and rot. The stench is already strong."

Lord Stanley choked, trying hard to hold back a laugh that he wasn't successful doing. "Yes. Well, it certainly seems something would be done sooner than later. You are right, he can't remain here for long."

Still clinging to Lord Stanley's hand, they both approached the table with the body that most likely was St. Clair. She began to shiver and instructed her body to behave itself. She was a strong woman. She had seen pictures that would cause most women, and even some men, to run for the chamber pot to relieve themselves of their last meal.

Lord Stanley's hand shook as he reached for the thin sheet covering the body. Slowly, he pulled it down, both gasping when St. Clair's face was revealed.

Without light, they had to look closely at his head. Luckily, their eyes had adjusted to the dark so they could see fairly well with the tiny bit of light coming through the windows.

"Here is where he hit his head." Stanley pointed to a mark on St. Clair's head. A puncture wound. "This looks to me as if he was pushed into the fireplace. Most likely at a pointed edge. See how deep the wound is? He hit it with some force."

Trying very hard to keep her last meal down, Marigold examined the wound, still holding her hand in front of her face, trying very hard not to breath. "Yes. I agree." Steeling herself, she leaned closer to the man's mouth and sniffed. She reared back and turned away, covered her mouth to keep everything that was inside where it should be.

"Why did you do that? The smell is bad enough."

"I didn't smell any alcohol near his mouth." With that statement, and feeling a bit steadier, she drew the sheet down and sniffed his clothing.

"Someone dumped alcohol on his clothes. But with no odor near his mouth, he was most likely killed and then whoever killed him splashed him with alcohol, so it would appear he tripped while drunk.

"Yes, that's what the police said."

They were both staring at the man when Marigold screamed as something hit her on the back of her neck.

CHAPTER SEVEN

Jonathan grabbed Marigold's flailing arms as she swatted at herself and continued to scream.

"Marigold! Stop screaming, they can probably hear you all the way in Bath."

She continued to slap at herself and shake uncontrollably. "Something hit me in the back of my neck."

Just then a very scraggly feral cat landed on the table, right next to St. Clair's head. They both jumped back as the animal hissed at them, its back arched, then chomped on the man's head and ran off with his toupee clamped between its teeth.

Marigold slumped against Jonathan. "Oh, my God. I shall never recover from this." He could see the pulse in her neck throbbing and she clutched her chest as if she were to collapse at any moment.

Completely rattled himself, he took a moment to compose himself, then grabbed her hand. "Let's leave. We've seen enough."

Marigold tugged his hand as he reached the

bottom of the stairs. "The sheet! We must cover St. Clair up, or they will know someone was in here."

He shook his head and continued. "No, they'll blame it on the blasted cat. Hopefully, right before they shoot it."

They raced up the stairs and into the room where they had entered the building. Jonathan shoved open the window and climbed out. He held up his arms. "Place your hands on my shoulders and I will lift you out."

Marigold did as he bid, and he lifted her, sliding her slowly down his body until her feet hit the ground. They were both panting as if they'd run a race—which they had. "Are you well?"

She turned and grabbed his hand, dragging him down the alley. "I've been better."

As if the hounds of hell were at their heels they made their way out of the alley and to the carriage sitting quietly at the curb. Jonathan slammed the door so smartly, the entire carriage rocked.

They'd been in the carriage for several minutes before their breathing returned to normal. "That was quite a fright." Jonathan viewed Marigold as they passed a street light. The poor girl's complexion was as white as new snow. "Are you sure you are well?"

She bent over, grasping her middle. "I will be fine in a moment. I believe my blood is not circulating to my head. I feel a bit lightheaded."

Leave it to a woman knowledgeable in anatomy to find a different way to say she was about to swoon. Jonathan joined her on her seat and rubbed her back as she continued to rest her forehead in her lap.

After a few minutes her breathing eased, and she slowly sat up. "Better." Her smile, combined with the tension of the evening, did something to his insides that had him acting so stupidly, he should have laughed. Had he been rational.

Instead, he ignored the warning voice in his head and leaned forward, wrapped his hand around Marigold's neck and pulled her forward until their lips joined.

A mistake. A very large mistake.

He wouldn't say bells went off, but his lower body parts certainly sang a sonata. Apparently, Marigold felt something too, because she all but crawled up his body as the kiss grew longer. She grasped his head and return his fervor.

Their lips met, withdrew. They moved their heads into different positions and resumed kissing. He nudged her lips with his tongue and she opened to him. Heaven. Her mouth was sweet, warm, and moist. He played with her tongue, and she entangled hers with his. Someone moaned, possibly both of them.

They had just gotten to the point where he'd shoved her pelisse from her shoulders and had unfastened the back of her gown when the carriage came to a halt. They both pulled back, horror growing in Marigold's eyes. "Oh, my."

"Indeed." Jonathan ran his fingers through his hair and backed up. Circling his finger in the air, he said, "Turn, and I will fasten your gown."

Not being a young, foolish, swooning miss, she did not ask how it had become unfastened. She had been an active participant, and had the carriage not arrived at her home when it had, he was afraid she would not have entered her home in the same virtuous state in which she'd left.

Taking a deep breath to calm the riotous lust racing through him, he helped her down and said, "I shall walk you round to the back."

"That is not necessary. I will be fine." Before he could respond, she pulled her pelisse tight against her body and hurried away. He watched until she'd made it to the door and then climbed back into his carriage.

It had been quite a night.

The following evening, Jonathan entered the Hayward ballroom where the event of the evening was taking place. He'd passed on an invitation to join several other bachelors on a trip to The Rose Room, the latest gambling hell to draw huge crowds each night. Owned by two brothers—although rumor had it a high-ranking peer was the financial backer—it had risen from a small, unknown club to the 'place to be' for gentlemen.

As expected, the minute his foot hit the floor in the ballroom, his eyes found Marigold. He no longer thought of her with the 'lady' title. Certainly not after what they'd shared in the morgue, and then in the carriage on the way to her house.

What he felt for her and where it might lead was something he did not wish to ponder. He still held out for a shy, biddable miss for a wife, quite unlike the outspoken, barely proper Marigold. However, with her being a gently reared daughter of an earl, an affair was out of the question.

He broke into a smile and headed directly for her when she looked from where she was having a conversation with some young pup and smiled at him. There was a definite invitation in that look.

"Good evening, Lady Marigold. May I say, you are looking quite lovely tonight." He bowed over her hand, glancing briefly at the card swinging from her wrist.

He turned to Lady Crampton, the only other woman in the group, and offered his greeting. Several men crowding around gave him surly looks. Looking back at Marigold, he said, "May I request a dance, my lady?"

***

Marigold preferred to not have Jonathan know she had saved the supper waltz for him, but once she extended her card, his eyes lit up, and he quickly scribbled his name. She hated how her face heated up at his touch, and hoped none of the gentlemen surrounding her, and especially Lady Crampton had not witnessed her fluster.

Instead of marching off, which is what she'd fully expected him to do, Jonathan—after their adventure to the morgue she could never again think of him as Lord Anything—continued to stay with the group. However, he only spoke to her or Lady Crampton. His dismissal of the other men was comical.

"My lady, I believe this is my dance." Lord Quimby bowed to her and extended his hand.

"If you will excuse me." She smiled at the men in the group and took Quimby's hand. He properly placed her hand on his forearm. No tingles in her center. No fluttering in her stomach. Although that hadn't surprised her since she had never felt the same thing with other gentlemen as she had with Jonathan. Even the men who had courted her and made her an offer of marriage.

That was disturbing and exciting at the same

time. She didn't mind being attracted to Jonathan, but she certainly didn't want to end up married to him. Although she'd learned his stiffness could soften at times, a lifetime with a man who still disapproved of her would be trying.

Perhaps an affair? Just the thought of it, as Lord Quimby clasped hands with her and swung her in a circle in time to the music, brought very strong flutters and tingles to her insides. Soon she would no longer be considered suitable for marriage, anyway, so why not have an affair? She had read enough on anatomy to know there were ways to prevent becoming with child. Did she have enough nerve to act on her attraction?

The thoughts of her and Jonathan continuing with what they'd started in the carriage, and how far it would go, kept her entertained the entire time she danced several sets with other gentlemen.

Finally, the man that had held her thoughts prisoner all evening approached her for their waltz. The look in his eyes as he placed his hand on her lower back and took her other hand in his, heated her so, she felt the need to whip out her fan and blow some cool air her way.

"Are you enjoying the ball, my dear?"

"Yes." Oh, for goodness sake, was that her voice? She sounded like one of those squeaky, squealing, giggling young misses. She cleared her throat. "Are you enjoying yourself, my lord?"

"I am now." He turned them in a circle, his skill on the dance floor remarkable. "Can we be finished with the 'my lady' and 'my lord?' It seems to me after all we've shared we can use our Christian names."

She nodded. "Yes, I find that acceptable. Do you

prefer Stanley or Jonathan?"

He bent low and practically whispered. "I'd love to hear Jonathan on your lips. Especially…" He stopped and grinned, his brown eyes smoldering. Had he not been holding her so securely, she would surely have mis-stepped and sent them both tumbling to the floor.

Despite what he did to her body with his voice and eyes, she had to keep reminding herself that she really didn't like the man. He was condescending, disapproving, and arrogant.

There. That should keep her body in control.

"Have you recovered from our adventure?"

Marigold shivered. "Yes. I must admit the one trip to the morgue was enough to satisfy my curiosity and allow me to move on with the study of anatomy without yearning to see another dead body."

"I think it is time for us to seriously discuss the situation. I think the viewing of St. Clair's body has convinced us he was murdered. I am also certain, especially now that we have ruled out an accidental death, that the journal is somehow connected."

"Yes. I believe I do have to agree with you on that. Had the man's death actually been accidental, then I wouldn't necessarily agree, but the journal turning up missing right after St. Clair is murdered definitely looks suspicious."

"We must find a place to be together to gather facts and devise a plan where we will not be overhead."

She mentally drew a check mark in Jonathan's favor for not dismissing her from the investigation. Maybe he wasn't so very condescending, arrogant, and disapproving as she had thought.

"You do understand we are solving a murder, as well as finding the journal?" Jonathan said.

"Yes." She raised her chin in the air. "And what do I get out of this, Jonathan? You get your journal back, but what do I get for my trouble?"

He grinned long enough to make her squirm. Whatever was going on in his devious mind?

"All right. When—and I will not say *if*—we retrieve the journal, I will allow you to look at it."

"Just look at it? Pshaw, that's no big reward. I want to be able to keep it for a while."

"Keep it?" His eyes almost bugged out of his head.

"Yes. I believe once this is over you will concede that we both own the journal."

He snorted "That I paid for."

"I will reimburse you half." She narrowed her eyes. "Since you were unable to hold onto it for even a whole day, I think I should be the primary owner, and you can borrow it from me."

Jonathan swept them right out the French doors, down the steps and into the dark garden.

CHAPTER EIGHT

Once they were in the garden, Jonathan wrapped his arm around Marigold's waist and hustled her to the nearest bench. When she was seated, he placed both hands on the bench alongside her hips and leaned in close. "What was it you just said to me, Lady Marigold?"

"I merely pointed out that your record for keeping the journal safe is not remarkable." She fussed with her skirts, not looking him in the eyes. "I think I should be the one to keep the journal and you can borrow it whenever you wish." She looked up at him, defiance in every feature, her lips so close he was almost distracted.

He truly did not know whether to laugh or throttle her. Since he was a gentleman, he elected to kiss her instead. In one quick motion, he swooped in, and pulled her to him, crushing her body to his, his mouth plundering hers. Ah, the sweetness he remembered. How could such a sweet mouth spew such nonsense?

She didn't even fight him, but again became a very enthusiastic participant. Just as he'd suspected from the very beginning, there was a lot of fire in this woman. And he wanted to be the one to unleash it. Preferably on a nice comfortable bed.

The sound of voices not too far from where they stood—ravishing each other like their ship was sinking—brought him back to time and place. Unless he wanted to be saddled with Marigold for the rest of his life, he'd best get her back to the ballroom before they created a scandal that could only end in marriage.

Not that the idea of marriage to her held as much distaste as it had at one time. The woman was certainly intelligent enough to give him a lifetime of lively debates. And her passion was very, very interesting, indeed. If only she didn't flirt disaster as much as she did.

Studying anatomy, insisting on accompanying him to the morgue, ordering magazines meant only for men. He wouldn't be surprised to learn she smoked cigars and drank brandy in her bedchamber at night.

But she did heat up his blood. He drew away from her kiss-swollen lips. Yes, she was a dangerous woman. "Someone is coming."

"Oh." She patted her hair, that was never tidy, anyway, and smoothed her gown. "It is best if we return to the ballroom. It is time for supper."

"Yes." He held out his arm and they walked the path to the French doors as if they had done no more than discuss the unusually pleasant weather.

"We did not discuss our next move." He spoke to her from the side of his mouth. "I shall collect you tomorrow around two o'clock for a ride in the park."

"Lady Crampton will have to accompany me."

He sighed, forgetting the annoyance of having a chaperone always breathing down their necks. As much as he liked Lady Crampton, he preferred Marigold all to himself. Which was precisely why she required a chaperone. "I will bring my phaeton. With it only seating two and it being an open carriage, there will be no need for a chaperone."

"I believe that will work." Marigold caught Lady Crampton's eye, who shook her head, letting Marigold know, he assumed, that she would not be joining them for supper, but would take her repast with one of her many friends. Once they arrived in the room where the food had been set out, Marigold took the seat Jonathan drew out for her.

"I shall return with some fare for us. Is there anything you particularly dislike?"

She scrunched her nose in the most adorable way. "Pickled herring."

"Hm. I don't imagine that will be one of the offerings, but that is good to know." He strolled off just as Lady Haskell took the seat next to Marigold. With Lord Haskell striding toward the table laden with numerous types of food, it appeared his opportunity to speak to Marigold by herself will have to wait for the next afternoon since their party of two just became a party of four.

He set two plates full of small sandwiches and sweets before him and took the seat across from Marigold. Placing his serviette on his lap, he turned to Lady Haskell. "Good evening, Lady Haskell. You are doing well?"

"Good evening to you as well, Lord Stanley. Yes, I am well."

Just then Lord Haskell joined the group, and the conversation continued, centered around events coming up, the latest play on Drury Lane, and the constant complaining about the weather. For a time, Marigold and Lady Haskell compared notes on fashion while Jonathan and Lord Haskell spoke of bills in parliament.

Once the meal had been consumed, the guests began to wander back to the ballroom, or card room, depending on their preferences. "Would you care to return to the ball, my lady?"

"Actually, I believe I am feeling fatigued. I will find Lady Crampton and make it an early night."

"Wait here, and I will find her for you, and request your carriage be brought around." He set off to find Marigold's chaperone, feeling quite cheerful at having spent time with Marigold, and taking it upon himself to make certain he was able to alert Lady Crampton that her charge wished to return home early.

He found Lady Crampton just returning to the ballroom with several of the women she seemed to gather with at each event. "My lady, Lady Marigold has expressed a desire to return home."

"Oh, Selina, please don't say you must leave just yet. We were about to invite you to make our fourth at whist." One of Lady Crampton's companions looked askance at her.

"Lady Crampton, if I may." Jonathan said. "I will be more than happy to escort Lady Marigold home."

"That is not appropriate. I need to see to her welfare."

He bowed in her direction, regretting not having the opportunity to spend more time with Marigold.

61

Alone. "As you wish, my lady. I will ask for your carriage to be brought around. I believe Lady Marigold awaits you in the supper room."

"Such a nice young man." One of her companions said as he walked off.

Yes. A nice young man feeling thwarted at not having a young unmarried miss all to himself in a dark carriage. He sighed and continued to the entrance hall to request her carriage.

***

Marigold double-checked her appearance in the looking glass behind her dressing table. The pale-yellow gown with small pink rosebuds embroidered around the neckline and hem brought out the gold in her hazel eyes. She pinched her cheeks and bit her lips, then laughed at herself. She was only going riding with Jonathan.

As she fussed with her ever trying hair, she thought about the two kisses they'd shared. It had been next to impossible to get him out of her mind. His strong arms as he'd held her, the citrusy scent that always surrounded him, and most of all his warm lips and lovely kisses. She sighed. Having an affair was not far from her mind these days. She knew various ways to prevent pregnancy, as she was sure Jonathan did as well.

She would probably never marry and have the need to explain her missing virginity to an outraged husband. She loved her sisters' children and doted on them as a loving aunt should. That would fulfill her need for children. The only thing standing between her and Jonathan enjoying intimate relations was his status as a gentleman.

All children of the aristocracy learned from the nursery a gentleman did not dally with a gently bred young lady. One dallied with opera dancers, willing widows, and courtesans as freely as one wished, but one married the well-bred ladies. There had been a few men who had crossed that line, and in addition to the young lady being disgraced, the men were not accepted as true gentlemen, and were, in some cases, actually shunned. Most men had sisters and did not like the idea that a man might do that to one of the ladies under their care and protection.

Marriage to Jonathan might not be as terrible as it would with another man who would most likely disparage her intelligence and try to push her into a role as his wife that she did not want to play. Jonathan seemed to respect her acumen and had even sought her opinion on things. That was, indeed, a rarity among men, whose general opinion was women were weak, unintelligent, swooning bundles of fluff.

A slight scratch on her door drew her attention from her meanderings to the young maid who stepped into the room. "Milady, Lord Stanley has arrived for your ride."

"Thank you, Jenny." Marigold picked up her shawl, bonnet, and gloves and left the room. She quickly made her way down the stairs to where Jonathan waited for her.

He looked remarkably well as he stood conversing with Macon. His hair had been slicked back, although a few strands were already staging a revolution and inched toward his broad forehead. A deep blue wool jacket outlined his shoulders and led one's eyes to the snug-fitting buff pantaloons and knee-high hessian boots. His blue and white print waistcoat set his outfit off quite nicely.

She grinned. Together they made a handsome couple.

"Good afternoon, Lord Stanley, I believe? Pomeroy, here." Papa popped out of nowhere—something he was apt to do—and extended his hand to Jonathan.

"Yes, my lord. It is a pleasure to meet you." Jonathan took his hand and they shook, both men eyeing each other.

Marigold rolled her eyes as she pulled on her gloves. Hopefully Papa would not invite Jonathan into his library as he'd done with her sisters' beaux when they'd first met. The thought panicked her that Papa might think Jonathan was a beau, since she rarely, if ever, took rides in the park with gentlemen. She had begun begging off on such trips once she realized all the men who had shown her interest would never suit with their narrow-mindedness.

Before he could drag Jonathan away, Marigold stepped up and took his arm. "Let us be on our way."

"Is Lady Crampton accompanying you?" Papa regarded them over the top of his spectacles.

"I am taking Lady Marigold on a ride in Hyde Park in my phaeton. Only room for two, you see, plus it is an open carriage. I do hope you approve?"

Papa waved his hand, giving Marigold a look that told her there would be a conversation about this ride once she returned. She hid a sigh as she took her parasol from Macon's hand. She enjoyed Jonathan's company, they had much in common, but she didn't want Papa pushing her toward the altar.

A few years ago, he had sat his three daughters

down and told them he would not accept marriage offers for his two youngest daughters, Juliet and Marigold, until his eldest, Elise was married. Since Elise had been a very happy spinster, it had thrown the entire family into a whirl. Elise eventually fell in love with Lord St. George, Juliet with Lord Hertford. They both had children and were happily settled.

While she had expected Papa to begin his campaign to get her married as soon as Juliet had walked down the aisle toward Lord Hertford, he had been somewhat derelict in his duty there. She and her sisters had discussed the matter and concluded that his lack of interest in marrying Marigold off was because of Lady Crampton.

Everyone knew Papa had feelings for the governess, and she for him. But no one mentioned it. Having Marigold still at home gave Papa a reason to keep Lady Crampton right there under his nose without making the major decision to marry her.

Shrugging off her thoughts about Papa and Lady Crampton, Marigold breathed in the warm spring air as they made their way to the phaeton. It was truly a lovely day to be riding in the park.

Jonathan helped her into the phaeton, then took his place next to her, picked up the ribbons and they started off.

"I want to have a serious discussion with you once we are on our way." Jonathan's words and demeanor brought Marigold to full attention.

CHAPTER NINE

The park was more crowded than Jonathan would have liked, but then he was not a huge fan of riding in Hyde Park during the fashionable hour where a good many of the Beau Monde were out in their finery, seeing and being seen. If a gentleman was escorting a lady on an afternoon ride gossip started, tongues wagged, heads turned, and mumbling behind fans began.

Nevertheless, he was happy to have Marigold by his side despite the number of vehicles to be maneuvered around, and the looks cast in their direction. Once he got them on a steady pace, he turned to her. "Since the police believe St. Clair died accidentally, and we know that to be untrue, we must do something about that. As well as find the journal."

"Perhaps we should go to the police and tell them our findings."

He leaned back and regarded her with raised brows. "And tell them what? That we broke into the morgue one night and examined the body?"

"Um, yes, I see your point. That would never do."

"No, it would not."

"Lady Marigold, how lovely to see you here today!" Mr. Dawson tipped his hat from where he sat atop his mount. The man had good taste in horseflesh, that was certain, although it was obvious his Akhal-Teke, with its golden gleam that caught the eye of everyone in the park, was more for attention. It stood at least fifteen hands, and tossed its beautiful head, anxious to be on its way.

"Good afternoon, Mr. Dawson," Marigold said. Jonathan merely nodded at the man, who returned his nod with a curt "Stanley."

Marigold blushed prettily and twirled her parasol. What the devil was that all about? She was flirting with the cur? Didn't she know that devil owed everyone in London? Rumor had it he hadn't even made good on his latest vowels, which no gentlemen neglected.

"We really need to move along, Lady Marigold. We are holding up the line." Jonathan snapped the ribbons and his horse moved forward.

"You know, perhaps I should ride more in the afternoon. I'd forgotten how pleasant it could be." Marigold looked around and smiled.

Jonathan scowled.

"My goodness, look who managed to get the lovely Lady Marigold into the park." Lord Lambert and Lord Hardy were next to annoy them.

"I've asked her ladyship to ride with me several times. What magic did you work, Stanley?" Hardy grinned at Marigold from his perch on his horse. Jonathan gave Marigold a quick glance, disliking how far down her bodice the man's position on his horse allowed him to view.

"No magic, maybe the lady is merely discerning in her selection of company."

Both men guffawed, bringing attention to them, which brought more men on horses over to their carriage. Jonathan shook his head in disgust. "We will never get around the park if this mob continues to grow, Marigold."

His riding partner ignored him as she bantered, flirted and teased one gentleman after another.

"Yoo-hoo, Lord Stanley." Jonathan turned to see Lady Humphries with her three unmarried daughters pull up alongside them in their landau. "It is so nice to see you out and about. We don't see you very often in the park."

Bloody hell, was he now going to be subjected to the marriage minded mamas and their silly, giggling daughters? This had not been the best of ideas. He wanted Marigold alone, so they could discuss their next move regarding the journal. As the crowds grew around them, it appeared it would be good fortune if they even circled the park one time.

"Good afternoon, ladies. It is a pleasure to see all of you as well." Jonathan bowed to the woman and her daughters, hoping they would move along.

"Lord Stanley, I am planning a lovely garden party next week. I know you received your invitation. I do hope you will join us. Lady Florence, my eldest, would love to have you attend."

Jonathan glanced in the direction of the said Lady Florence who scowled in his direction. Her mother took notice and gave her a sharp command. The girl immediately dipped her head and smiled. "I would love for you to join us, my lord."

"I will check my calendar. If I am free, it would be my pleasure to join you."

Lady Humphries gloated, and he had the sinking feeling she was planning the wedding breakfast. He shuddered. The three young girls in the carriage were precisely the type he'd been avoiding for years. Young, silly, nothing in their heads, and more than ready to leg shackle a man.

"Lady Marigold we really must move on." It was getting harder and harder to keep from pulling a few of the men practically drooling over Marigold from their horses and beating the airheads bloody.

She waved at the gentlemen, and with calls to her for promised dances, they left her side, giving Jonathan room to finally move the carriage. "You must discontinue encouraging these men."

Marigold looked over at him, eyebrows raised. "What is the problem, my lord?"

Uh, oh, they were back to 'my lord.' "There is no problem, it is just that we were holding up the line, and I did want to speak with you about the journal and what our course of action should be."

Marigold smoothed her gown. "I am sorry if there were people who wish to speak with me."

He guided the horse around a couple on foot, walking slowly. "Not people. Men."

"Oh, how horrible!" She twirled her parasol so enthusiastically, he was afraid it would hit him in the head. "What if I am popular with the men? I did nothing wrong."

"Only leading them on."

She scowled. "What is that supposed to mean?"

He continued to stare at the horses as they

moved closer to the exit from the park. "It means you've told me more than once you don't find most men suitable because of their attitude toward women."

"Yes. These men," she waved around the park, "are mostly idiots."

"Then why encourage them?"

"Because it is fun. Because I enjoy it. Because, even though I have my more serious side, I also take pleasure in joy and laughter." She turned her back to him and tossed over her shoulder, "Unlike others I know who think having a bit of fun is somehow improper."

***

Marigold fumed as they made their way out of the park. Where did Lord Arrogant get the idea he could comment on her behavior? Just because he was a scowling, grumpy man didn't mean she had to adopt his demeanor.

Of course, she could not just continue to sit there and not have her say. Men might be able to fume in silence, but rarely women. "If we are speaking of flirting, my lord, perhaps you can delve into your memory and shake the dust off the image of the lovely Lady Frances making cow eyes at you."

"Cow eyes?" He snorted. "She was scowling in my direction until her mother snapped at her."

"Well, after that, she certainly seemed happy to chat with you. She was giggling and batting her eyes, and generally looking the fool." She spun her parasol, almost making herself dizzy. When the houses they passed seemed to dip and sway, she stopped the twirling and grasped the edge of the phaeton.

"Are you well, Marigold?" Jonathan regarded her with concern.

"Yes. I am fine." At least she was fine now that she stepped off the carousel.

"I can assure you, I did not notice any batting of eyelashes, although I must admit there seemed to be a great deal of giggling going on. Not just from Lady Frances, but from her two sisters as well."

"And don't forget Lady Humphries practically falling out of her carriage trying to get your attention when they first drove up." Marigold clamped her mouth shut. She sounded like a shrew. A jealous shew. Which was nonsense since she had no reason whatsoever to feel jealous of any woman who paid attention to Jonathan.

They were merely friends. Partners in business, practically. Cohorts in their study of anatomy.

When they pulled up to her house, Jonathan turned and faced her. "Please accept my apologies for my grousing. It is just that I had hoped to speak with you privately."

"Well, I guess we discovered 'privately' does not go well with riding in Hyde Park at the fashionable hour. I apologize for my grumpiness as well."

"Accepted." He jumped down and walked to the other side to help her from the carriage. "Will you be attending the literary society meeting this evening?"

"Yes, I planned on it."

They made their way up the stairs where Macon already had the door open.

"Excellent. May I call for you at seven o'clock? Lady Crampton is more than welcome to ride with us."

"She doesn't usually attend the meetings with me. On the nights we don't have *ton* events to attend, she enjoys remaining at home in the library, doing her sewing while Papa reads. I don't think there will be a problem with me riding with you since I attend these meetings all the time."

"Very well. Then we will have time to discuss all the journal situation on our way there." He bowed over her hand as he took his leave.

Several hours later, they were in Jonathan's closed carriage, the familiar clopping of the horses' hooves on the cobblestones creating a soothing rhythm. The lanterns next to their heads cast a golden glow over them as the carriage made its way to the meeting. Marigold had long since lost her pique with Jonathan, as was her nature. She was never able to remain angry for long.

"What is this plan you have come up with?" She shifted in her seat and grabbed onto the strap as the carriage rocked over uneven ground.

"Since the list for the estate sale was presented at the meeting, I believe the person who stole the book is a member of the society. Perhaps he tried to purchase it after I left and when he found this out, broke into my home and took it."

"How does that figure into killing St. Clair, though? He no longer had the journal."

"That is true, and something to be considered, of course. I think our purpose this evening should be to speak with some of the members. Ask about their reaction to St. Clair's death. I imagine the news is all over London now, and would be of special interest to the Society members since some of them may have attended the estate sale and met St. Clair."

"I agree. I know we are both anxious to find the journal—which will be held in my safekeeping from now on—but finding a murderer and turning him over to the police would be quite satisfying."

"Um, excuse me, Lady Marigold? Did I just hear you say the journal will be—how did you phrase it?—safe in your keeping from now on?"

She regarded him wide-eyed. "I thought we agreed on that."

"We did not. When you stated those preposterous words, I kissed them away."

His smirk and the burning in his eyes, visible from the lantern by his head, caused Marigold to suck in a deep breath. Hearing him refer to their kiss in such a casual way affected the beating of her heart until she was sure Jonathan could hear it.

He took her hand in his large, warm one and leaned forward. "Something I would like to repeat soon." His lowered voice and soft tone melted her insides.

Maybe the two of them riding together in his coach without Lady Crampton had not been such a good idea after all. She inched further on her seat. Nonsense. Kissing in a dark carriage was a very fine thing to do.

And a great idea.

CHAPTER TEN

Despite Jonathan and Marigold never having conversed a great deal during the literary society meetings in the past, no undue attention was given to them when they arrived together. Jonathan had laid out the plan to Marigold that they should gravitate toward those with whom they normally conversed, bring up the subject of the man who ran the estate sale dying unexpectedly, and carefully watch what sort of reactions they received.

Thankfully—or not, depending on what his head said and what his lower parts screamed out—once Marigold edged toward him in the dark carriage, and he didn't resist kissing her, the vehicle soon drew up to the meeting place. The one kiss they'd managed to get in left him reeling, and fully ready for more.

The ride home might be quite interesting. But then again, they did need to behave themselves enough that they could move forward in their search for the journal and murderer. Also, he needed to continue to remind himself that despite the very strong attraction between them, he saw little in their future.

Even if he were to overlook Lady Marigold's propensity to appear flighty and her need to delve into areas no lady should be tempted toward, he had no idea what she would think of a marriage between them.

Marriage? He broke into a sweat. Had he reached the point where he wanted her so much he was willing to step into the vicar's noose to get her into his bed? What he should be considering was getting his journal back and letting things cool between them. Marigold had already turned down any number of men, and he had no reason to believe she would accept him.

"Good evening, Lord Stanley. I'm anxious to hear your opinion on our latest book." Mr. Bentley slapped him on the back, moving him several inches forward and almost knocking him off his feet. The man was built like a tree trunk. Tall, wide, and large all over. Deep voice, black as night unruly hair. His sweeping mustache covered most of his face, a total comical contrast to the tiny spectacles resting on his large, bulbous nose.

The latest book? Jonathan startled when he realized with all the goings on since the last meeting, not only had he not read the required book for tonight's meeting but didn't even remember which one it was. "Er, yes. Interesting book, for sure. Quite interesting. Quite."

Bentley nudged him with his massive elbow, most likely bruising him in such away he would need an ice compress as he prepared for bed. "I said to my wife when I returned home from the last meeting that

Lord Stanley would certainly appreciate this book." He threw his head back and roared with laughter.

Bloody hell. If the others were going to look to him for opinions, he would appear a dimwit. "If you will excuse me, Bentley, I have to speak with Lady Marigold about something." With the man's guffaws echoing in his ears, Jonathan hurried across the room and grasped Marigold's elbow as she stood speaking with Mrs. Bentworth. "May I have a word, Lady Marigold?"

She turned to him, her brows raised. Before she could ask him what he wanted, he nodded to Mrs. Bentworth. "A pleasure to see you this evening, Mrs. Bentworth, That is a lovely hat. Very good color for you. If you will excuse us, I need to ask Lady Marigold something."

He dragged her off to the opposite corner of the room. Marigold pulled her elbow from him and tugged the cuffs of her sleeves. "Whatever is the matter with you? Mrs. Bentworth and I were talking about St. Clair. I believe she was about to tell me something of import."

"Well, you can continue that conversation later. I have a much more important question." He whispered the words, not wanting the entire room to hear of his lapse.

She bent her head toward him. "What is that?"

"Did you read the book for our meeting tonight?"

"Of course." She narrowed her eyes. "Didn't you?"

He ran his fingers through his hair, and then realizing Mrs. Bentworth continued to stare in their direction, he dropped his hand and smiled at

Marigold as if everything was wonderful, and they were discussing no more than the next social event, and his opportunity to secure a dance. "No, I did not. With everything that's gone on, it slipped my mind."

"Oh, dear. I would imagine they expect you to have quite an opinion on the book."

Bloody hell. "What *was* the book?"

"*Statement of the Question of Parliamentary Reform.* Mr. George Grote's book."

His jaw dropped that he could forget that book of all things. "Blast it all. I wanted to read that book, too."

"Language, Lord Stanley. I'm sure you did want to read it since you have such a keen interest in parliament. Furthermore, I'm sure they expect you to lead the meeting."

He groaned. "What am I to do?" He pulled out his watch fob. "We only have about fifteen minutes until the meeting begins."

She shook her head, and regarded him as if she were his governess, and he'd forgotten to do an important assignment. "Why I feel the need to take pity on a man when men have so little regard for a woman's intelligence, is probably worth a study in itself."

"Marigold. You know I hold you, and your intelligence, in high regard." He hoped she did not hear the pleading in his voice, only the sincerity of his words. He had truly grown to appreciate her intellect.

She studied him for a minute. "All right. Since I am such a very nice person, I will give you my opinion on the book."

Jonathan held his hand up. "Wait a minute, I don't want your opinion, I want to know what the book was about."

Marigold raised her chin and offered him a slight, devilish smile. "It is either *my* opinion, my lord, or *no* opinion at all."

***

Marigold thoroughly enjoyed having Jonathan at her mercy. Not that she was a mean person by nature, but for some inexplicable reason, she loved teasing him. He was so pompous at times, and so arrogant in his know-it-all attitude that she loved watching him squirm.

All right. Perhaps she did have her mean side.

She barely got the information out before Lord Dunkirk called the meeting to order. As per their plan, she and Jonathan went their separate ways and sat on opposite sides of the room. She was impressed more than she wanted to be when he led the meeting on the book. He managed to put out her opinions but made them seem as his own.

Smart man.

Once they were settled in the carriage and on their way to her house, Jonathan pulled a blanket out from under his seat and handed it to her. "It's grown quite chilly with the rain, you might as well be warm. I asked the driver to go slowly so we can discuss whatever information we have gleaned."

Of course, Marigold could think of several other ways they could keep warm, but since Jonathan seemed to be all business, and excited to tell her something, she tamped down her disappointment.

"I take it from your demeanor that you are not only pleased at having bamboozled the members of the society on how much you enjoyed the book we just discussed, and never read, but you have information for me on the journal."

"Yes. And I didn't bamboozle them." He winked at her. "I had a very intelligent woman prepare me for the discussion."

She felt the heat rise to her cheeks. "Well done, Lord Stanley."

Jonathan leaned forward. "It turns out Dr. Paglia had a partner, cohort, whatever one wishes to call him. They worked together on some of the discoveries that Paglia is credited with. From what I was told this evening by Mr. Wedgewood, who seemed to be quite familiar with the story, Dr. Paglia, and his partner, Dr. Stevenson parted ways about five years ago for unknown reasons."

Marigold sat back and considered what he'd just said. "That is quite interesting, indeed."

"What is even more interesting is Dr. Stevenson returned to England from an extensive visit abroad very soon after Dr. Paglia died."

"Did he travel to the continent after their break?"

"Wedgewood seemed to think so. It was discussed in their circles that their falling out had something to do with their work together, although that was never fully determined. Soon after the break, Dr. Paglia retired to his estate in Cornwall where he spent the last years of his life."

"Writing in his journal." Marigold digested all that information, leading her to a question. "Were any other findings attributed to Dr. Paglia after his break with Dr. Stevenson?"

Jonathan looked at her with a new sense of

respect. "You are thinking precisely what I was thinking. That perhaps the discoveries credited to Dr. Paglia were actually the work of Stevenson."

"That did cross my mind. Did you find out if there were?"

Jonathan shrugged. "A few others, but nothing as notable as the ones recorded during the years they shared their partnership."

Marigold stared out the window of the carriage at the rain sliding down the glass. The inside of the carriage had grown misty with their breaths. They seemed to be cocooned in their own little world. "Yet, if the journal ended with Dr. Paglia's death, no one knew of its existence until the new Lord St. Clair inherited the estate and put things up for sale."

"That's correct. Yet, Dr. Stevenson has been here all this time. More than a year."

"Does he still delve into anatomy, do you know?"

"Not that I've seen. I haven't heard of him at all in fact. You are as much involved in the study as I am. Have you heard of him before tonight?"

Marigold shook her head.

They sat in silence for a while, then Jonathan shifted to rest his foot on his bent knee. "This is what I propose. I suggest we visit with Dr. Stevenson and engage him in conversation about anatomy, and how excited we were to discover he worked with Dr. Paglia and all this time he was right here in London."

"You won't be able to go. If he did, in fact, steal the journal, then he will recognize your name, and won't be willing to receive us."

"I have thought of that. Dr. Stevenson does not move about in Society. He is not a peer. There is no way he would recognize me. I will merely give a false name when I send a note around to ask for a meeting."

Despite asking for a slow ride to Marigold's house, the carriage soon stopped its forward motion and the driver jumped down. She was disappointed that they didn't share a kiss. She was certainly becoming wanton!

Jonathan stepped out and turned to assist her down. "I will send a note around to Stevenson's house tomorrow morning. I have some stationery from Lord Applegate when he visited me a few years ago. That should work fine. As soon as I have an answer as to what time we may call, I will notify you."

Marigold smiled and took his arm as they ascended the steps. Macon had the door open, which allowed for no private conversation to continue. She turned to him as they stepped into the entrance hall. "Thank you for escorting me, Lord Stanley."

He bowed over her hand. "It was my pleasure, I assure you."

"Stanley! Good to see you, young man. I'd like to have you join me for a brandy before you hurry away." Papa's joviality had Marigold cringing. Lady Crampton followed behind him, a smirk on her face as she regarded Marigold.

"Yes, of course, my lord. I would love to join you in a brandy." Jonathan ran his finger along the inside of his cravat and followed Papa down the corridor to the library.

CHAPTER ELEVEN

Jonathan followed Lord Pomeroy down the corridor to the library. He did not feel as nervous as he thought he should. He knew what Marigold's father wanted to speak about. Most fathers would want to have a word with a man who had been escorting his daughter out on rides in Hyde Park and to evening meetings.

His only concern was what he planned to say to Lord Pomeroy if he flat out asked what his intentions were. He didn't know the man very well, since his lordship did attend some *ton* events, but generally was known to head directly to the card room.

"Here, take a seat, young man. I assume you're a brandy drinker?" Pomeroy motioned toward a chair in front of the fireplace. At least he hadn't been directed to the chair across from his desk which would have seemed more like an interview.

"Yes, brandy is fine. Thank you."

Once they were settled with their drinks, Pomeroy wasted no time. "I've seen you a couple of times lately. Rides in the park, and what not. Lady Crampton tells me you appear to be dancing attendance on my lovely daughter."

"I find Lady Marigold very intelligent, witty, and of a pleasant demeanor." That should satisfy any father. Especially since he'd left out desirable, sensuous, and bloody damn tempting. No need to share that bit of information.

"Yes, she is a lovely girl. My youngest. Always held a special place in my heart. As did all three of my daughters. True blessings from their dear, departed mother." He made the sign of the cross. Funny, Jonathan hadn't known they were Catholic.

"Am I to assume you are interested in courting my daughter?"

Well, then. Let us cut right to the chase.

The question he needed to tread carefully with. Was he courting Marigold? It had not started that way. In fact, when they'd both played tug of war with the journal at the St. Clair estate sale, he could barely tolerate the chit. That was before he learned there was so much more to Lady Marigold than fluff and nonsense.

On the other hand, courting generally led to marriage proposals. Frankly, he was not thinking along those lines. Well, perhaps the thought had popped up a time or two, but he still had strong reservations about Marigold's suitability as his wife. And he had no idea how she would react to a proposal from him. She'd made it quite clear that she'd found the men who had courted her in the past wanting. He decided honesty was the best policy.

"I admire your daughter quite a bit, and we enjoy spending time together. We are both members of the literary society, you know." There, that might push him toward another track.

Like a damn bloodhound, though, Pomeroy took a sip of his drink and viewed him over the rim of the glass. "Ah, the literary society. Her elder sister, the lovely Lady St. George was a member of the organization."

Jonathan held his breath because the shrewd man across from him was not finished, he was sure.

"And, at the time I was quite anxious to marry her off. A bluestocking. Confirmed spinster. Wanted to spend the rest of her life managing me." He shook his head. "I told my girls they had to marry in birth order, you know. I would never have gotten rid of Elise any other way."

Perhaps realizing how that sounded, the man quickly added, "Not that I didn't want my cherished daughters with me forever. It was simply time for them to have their own household. Manage husbands' lives. Set up their nurseries, that sort of thing. Wonderful creatures, daughters. Once they're off your payroll, they provide you with charming grandchildren."

"I understand."

"Good. I just wanted you to know I am in no hurry to lose my last treasured daughter."

Well, that was a turnaround. Most fathers were anxious to marry off their daughters what with all the expenses of a Season year after year. And given how many Seasons Marigold had passed, he found Pomeroy's words puzzling.

"I am glad to hear that, my lord."

As soon as the words passed his lips, he wished them back. He certainly didn't want it to appear he was trifling with the girl. Pomeroy, the clever man, smiled. "So, you've no wish to marry?"

Blast it all. How does one answer that question when one is semi-courting the man's daughter? "I wish to assure you my intentions are honorable, my lord. I would never do anything to jeopardize Lady Marigold's good name."

"Ah, well said. But that didn't answer my question."

He swallowed and glanced longingly at his empty brandy glass. "Of course, I will marry one day. I need an heir, after all. But I am in no hurry." Lord, he was getting himself in deeper and deeper. It appeared he didn't need a shovel to bury himself, just his mouth. "I know you might wonder why I am passing time with Lady Marigold."

Pomeroy nodded.

Now what was he to say? *We were fighting over the same journal when I wrangled it away from her, but it was stolen, and then we went to the morgue in the middle of the night and looked at a dead body? Oh, and I've kissed her a couple of times and imagine her naked when I fall asleep at night?*

Unless he came up with something brilliant he may never be welcome into this house again. "What I am having a difficult time saying, my lord, is I am fond of Lady Marigold. I enjoy her company and wish to spend time with her. If that leads to more than a mere companionship, I will certainly seek you out before I speak to her about anything permanent."

Jonathan heaved a sigh of relief when Pomeroy smiled and held up his glass. "I find that acceptable, young man. How about another brandy?"

Yes, indeed. He could certainly use one.

***

Marigold tamped down the nervous quivers in her stomach as she and Jonathan approached Dr. Stevenson's house. He lived in a quiet section of London. Not upper class, but solidly middle class. Merchants and such who didn't have enough money yet to buy their way into the aristocratic neighborhoods owned quite a few of the well-kept homes here.

"I believe I will take the lead in the conversation," Jonathan said as they mounted the steps to the doctor's home.

Ordinarily she would argue the point at his highhandedness, but she was far too anxious to dwell on that. They were about to speak to a man who could very well have killed Lord St. Clair and stolen the journal from Jonathan's house. It was hard to accept a man such as Dr. Stevenson, who worked so closely with the revered Dr. Paglia would do such a thing, but right now he was their only suspect.

The door was opened by a young maid, with slicked-back red hair and a face full of freckles. Her bright smile revealed a chipped tooth as she gave a slight dip. "Good morning, my lord, my lady, Dr. Stevenson is expecting you in the drawing room."

"Thank you." Since she was the only person in the front entrance hall, they handed over their hats, cane, and outerwear to her, which she deposited on a red and blue striped velvet chair and led them up the stairs to the drawing room.

Marigold's first impression of the man was that he could never have done such devious things. He was, as expected, an older man. On the short side, rotund, with flushed cheeks and a long mane of white hair. Clean shaven, he'd elected to sport white bushy sideburns.

He looked like someone's doting grandpapa.

"Good afternoon, Lord Applegate, Lady Marigold. Won't you have a seat?" He waved to a settee in front of a small table where tea service had been set up.

"Thank you, doctor." Once they were settled, Jonathan began. "We greatly appreciate you seeing us. It is truly a pleasure to meet you."

He dipped his head. "It is quite seldom I receive visitors at all. You mentioned in your note that you and the lady are both members of the Gentlemen and Ladies Literary Society of London, is that correct?"

"Yes, we are." Jonathan adjusted his jacket as he settled into his seat.

"Lady Marigold, will you pour, please?" Dr. Stevenson gestured toward the tea set.

"Yes. Of course." She took the teapot with shaky hands and willed herself to bring her body under control. Even if the man had committed murder, Jonathan was prepared with a dagger strapped to his calf and a pistol in his pocket. She had to admit she was more nervous about him accidentally shooting himself or her than any criminal. However, he had scoffed when she mentioned that and assured her he was well trained, and a crack shot.

She poured the tea, fixing each man's cup as they wished, then passed around the delightful looking sweets. Finally, once they were all settled, Dr. Stevenson took a sip of tea and then leaned back in his chair. "So, to what do I owe the pleasure of this visit? I assume it has something to do with the Society, since your note stated you are both members? I am not a member, never have been. Always wanted to join, don't you know?"

Marigold took a deep breath and tried hard not to fidget with her gown as Jonathan leaned forward. "Lady Marigold and myself are quite interested in the study of the human body."

The doctor's brows rose, and his eyes slid toward Marigold. She gave him a slight smile. "I know that is not a proper course of study for a woman, doctor, but I have never been prone toward the typical."

"Obviously." He grinned, his face resembling more with each moment a grandpapa who always had small candies hidden somewhere on his person for the little ones to tease out of him.

Jonathan cleared his throat. "It just came to our attention recently that you were in a partnership of sorts with the late Dr. Vincenzio Paglia."

Gone was the jovial, sociable man. In his place was a completely different person than the one from only a few seconds past. He drew back, his bushy brows drawn tightly over his forehead. He placed his tea cup on the table and crossing his arms over his massive belly, glared at them. Even his eyes had changed from sparkling and happy and was now dark and cautious. The change was remarkable. "I do not speak of Dr. Paglia."

Jonathan looked flummoxed. "Oh, I see. Did your partnership end unhappily?"

"I do not speak of Dr. Paglia." Instead of his voice rising, his tone grew deeper, and perhaps even a bit sinister.

Marigold looked over at Jonathan who returned

her puzzled expression.

"Have you been doing your own work on anatomy, then, Dr. Stevenson?"

The man abruptly stood, knocking over his tea cup that had been sitting on the edge of the table. "If you will excuse me, I have matters to which I must attend. My maid will see you out."

Before they could say anything else, the man turned on his heels, and for an older, bulky man made a quick exit from the room.

After a few stunned moments, Marigold whispered. "Well, then."

"Indeed," Jonathan returned.

Just then the maid appeared at the doorway, out of breath, leading them to believe she had been racing up the stairs. Most likely at her employer's behest. "I will show you out, my lord, my lady."

Nothing else to do, they both stood and followed her down the stairs. She handed them their belongings, and before they even were able to put them on, she opened the door and waved in a manner that suggested they should do whatever it was they felt they needed to do on the other side of the door.

The latch snapped shut and they both stood on the steps, holding various garments in a bundle and stared at each other. "That went well, don't you think?" Jonathan said.

CHAPTER TWELVE

They were both silent on the return ride to Marigold's house. Jonathan continued to be confused by Dr. Stevenson, and his behavior, going over in his mind their very brief meeting.

"What now?" Her soft voice broke into Jonathan's thoughts.

He regarded her, not sure if he should tell her his next move, because she would want to be involved, and he did not want her involved. "I will break into Stevenson's house and search for the journal."

A huge smile covered her face. "We will?"

Bloody hell, the woman had no sense of propriety or safety. "I said *I* will break in. There is no reason for you to go."

She looked almost as if she wanted to stamp her foot like a child. "I went to the morgue."

He waved his hand. "That was different."

"How so?" Her chin rose, and she regarded him with tight lips.

Jonathan took a deep breath, annoyed at having

to explain the situation because he was absolutely certain she would not accept his reasoning, and an argument would ensue. "I allowed you to go to the morgue—"

"—allowed me!" She did stamp her foot.

"—because you have some knowledge of anatomy."

She narrowed her eyes and her voice lowered. "Some knowledge?"

"Yes." He studied her tense position. "Very well. A great deal of knowledge." 'Twas best to stay on her good side if he hoped to pull this off without her joining in.

"That's better."

"This break-in is for the sole purpose of finding the journal. I will have it back—"

"—which we will keep in my possession."

He scowled. "—and then we can go to the police with evidence of the thievery and possible connection to St. Clair's death. I don't know that they would look again at his demise because we found—or stole—the missing journal. However, they probably would consider it since he was a peer. Ordinarily, the police don't dismiss a peer's possible murder."

"Yes, it would be highly irregular of them to dismiss a murder of a peer. Except St. Clair was new to London and had no family members clamoring for justice. I imagine the search for his successor will take up whatever time and resources his solicitors would have spent demanding better answers from the police. So, when do we go?"

Jonathan rolled his eyes. "Marigold, I really don't want you involved. You saw how quickly Stevenson turned on us when we mentioned his association with

Dr. Paglia. There is something sinister there, and it convinces me even more that he stole the journal. Why else would he be so adamant about not speaking of his former partner?"

She tapped her chin. "There was something strange about how his demeanor changed so abruptly. I still think I should go because with two of us we can search faster. Get in, get the journal, get out."

He would try one more time, but knew it was useless since Lady Marigold Smith was one of the most stubborn women he had ever met. "I can search quickly by myself if I know you are home safe, and not where you could be in danger."

She didn't bother to answer, just crossed her arms over her body and glared at him. "I am going. And don't try to go without me."

He had thought of doing that—sneaking out—but the repercussions did not seem worth the subterfuge. Lady Marigold was a determined woman, and he wouldn't put it past her to stake herself outside his home, waiting for him to go so she could trail him. Blast her father for being so lenient with her. She really ought to marry and have a husband take her in hand.

That thought didn't sit well with him at all. The image of another man taking her to his bed to enjoy the pleasures to be had with her body made him want to punch something.

"Very well," he conceded. "I had thought about going tonight. Since we never mentioned the journal during our very brief visit, Stevenson has no reason to believe our calling on him was no more than curiosity about how he and Dr. Paglia conducted their work. If we give him too much time to consider it, he might connect our visit to the journal and take efforts to secure it."

Marigold nodded. "But he stole it from you."

"Actually, after meeting Dr. Stevenson, I believe he had someone steal it for him. I can't imagine him climbing through a window in my library."

"True, and yes, tonight is best. What time?"

Jonathan sighed again. "Do you really want to put yourself in that position?"

"What I do want is for you to stop trying to dissuade me. I am going." She pointed her finger at him just as the carriage stopped in front of her house.

Shaking his head, Jonathan left the carriage, turned to help her down. "Two o'clock in the morning. Be dressed in dark clothes and do something with your hair to cover it up. There will be a moon tonight, and your hair will be quite visible."

"Yes, very good idea. I will be ready." The excitement in her voice rattled him. She would be death of him, yet.

"How will you get out of the house?"

"The same way I did when we went to the morgue. I told Lady Crampton I was under the weather and wished to retire early. Then when everyone was abed, I crept down the back stairs and met you."

He nodded his head, once again reminded how difficult a wife Marigold would be. Lord, if they married he would have to sleep with her tied to his wrist. That brought up other images that warmed him and had his lower parts coming to life.

***

"What the devil have you done?" Jonathan glared at Marigold as she exited the back door. It was two o'clock in the morning, and she was ready to accompany him on their quest to find the journal.

"What do you mean?"

"What do I mean? You are wearing breeches and have some sort of smudges on your face."

Marigold looked down at herself, hiding her smile. "Yes. I believe you are correct. I am wearing breeches."

Jonathan leaned his head back as if appealing to a higher power to give him strength. "What if someone sees you in those..." He waved in the general direction of her legs.

"Jonathan. We are about to break into a man's home and steal something from him. I think our main concern should be avoiding getting caught, not how I am dressed."

Breeches! Looking at her long legs encased snugly in men's trousers almost had him dragging her to the bushes to peel them off her slender form and have his way with her enticing body. She was enough of a temptation without making it harder on his overwrought man parts.

She continued to smile at him, as if she knew where his thoughts were wandering. He needed to get himself under control. They had a job to do. "And your face?"

"You said there would be a moon tonight. Therefore, I smeared a bit of coal on my face to cut down on the glow from my skin."

He took her by the elbow and moved her along. "Do you have any idea what those breeches do to me?"

"Do to you?"

"Yes. You don't want to know what I'm imagining as I look at your legs in those breeches." If he wasn't afraid of stumbling and throwing them both to the ground, he would close his eyes. Although that would not help since the image was already seared into his memory. Forever.

She grinned, enjoying his discomfort. "You don't say? How interesting."

"Stop it, Marigold," he snapped. "We have to keep our minds on what we are about to do."

"I have no problem doing that." She smirked.

"Fine. When we reach Stevenson's house, I will remove my jacket, waistcoat, and shirt and strut around his library."

"Oh." She flushed, the image of his bared torso, all that golden flesh gleaming in the moonlight dried up her mouth. How she would love to see that sight and run her fingers over his warm skin. "You win. Maybe the breeches were not a good idea."

By the time they settled the matter of the breeches and golden torso, the carriage was within proximity of Stevenson's house. They parked the carriage some distance away to avoid the possibility of attracting Stevenson's attention.

Marigold pushed the dark curtain aside and looked down the street toward the forbidding house. She shivered, thinking maybe she should have let him do this alone. "How will we get in?"

"I will try all the lower floor windows while you wait in the carriage. Then I will summon you when we can enter. I'm hoping one of the unlocked windows will be in the library. That way we won't have to stumble around the house, looking for the right room."

She watched him walk away, still imagining his naked chest. She huffed. 'Twas quite unfair of him to put that picture in her mind.

About ten minutes after he left her, he was back. "There is an open window in the library. We must hurry. I made a bit of noise when I came through the window and waited to see if anyone came to investigate. Luckily, no one did, but now I just want to get this over with." He held out his hand. "Come."

Hand-in-hand they made their way down the alley to the back of the house where a window was fully open. He twirled his finger to signal she should turn. Then he grabbed her around the waist and lifted as if she weighed no more than a bag of feathers. She rested her bottom on the window sill, then swung her legs in, and placed her feet as quietly as possible on the floor.

It was dark. Very dark. And an odd smell that she hadn't noticed when they were there earlier assailed her nostrils. She turned as Jonathan made it through the window.

He adjusted his clothing from the climb, then leaned close to her ear. "Let's split up. I will go through the bookshelves while you search the desk. There should be enough light from the moon that we won't need to light a candle. Even if the need arises, it shouldn't be a problem since we are at the back of the house, so no one from the street will see the candlelight."

Jonathan headed toward the closest book shelf and ran his fingers over the bindings. Marigold walked to the desk and drew open the middle drawer. Nothing but papers and old envelopes, some not even opened.

She looked in the drawer on her left, and her nose began to twitch. She rubbed it, hopefully avoiding a sneeze. Carefully she closed the drawer and reached for the one under it. Nothing there, either, but more papers, a ledger of some sort, and an ink well. Dr. Stevenson was certainly a messy man. But something was bothering her nose again. An unusual smell, almost metallic.

After moving to the other side of the desk, the smell got stronger. She passed the desk and looked alongside it. She gasped, and attempted to call Jonathan, but her throat froze. When it did open, she screamed.

Jonathan raced to where she was. "Marigold, for heaven's sake, be quiet. Dr. Stevenson will hear you and be down in a minute."

She continued to stare in horror and shook her head. "No."

"No, what?"

"Dr. Stevenson won't hear us, because Dr. Stevenson is lying at my feet with a very ugly knife protruding from his back." With those few words, her eyes rolled up in the back of her head and she slumped toward the floor.

"Marigold!" Jonathan dove for her.

CHAPTER THIRTEEN

Jonathan broke into a sweat as he heard footsteps on the stairs at the front of the house. He tapped Marigold's cheek. "Wake up, Marigold."

Nothing.

He eyed the French doors in between the two windows. Carrying Marigold in his arms, he strode to the door, unlatched it and left. It didn't matter that he left the door open because once the staff member on his way entered the library and saw the dead body of his employer that would take up his attention.

Unless, of course, one of the male servants had a pistol, in which case he might come after them, assuming they were the murderers. Hugging her close to his body to keep from jerking her too much, he raced to the carriage.

Surprising the driver, the man jumped down and quickly opened the door. "Hurry, get this vehicle moving." Juggling Marigold, Jonathan climbed into the carriage. "My house, but go to the mews, not the front entrance."

"Yes, my lord." He scurried to the top of the carriage and within seconds of the door closing they were rattling over the cobblestones. Jonathan looked behind him, but no one was chasing the carriage.

He returned his attention to Marigold. "Marigold. Wake up sweetheart." Why wasn't she a normal woman who would carry a vinaigrette in her reticule, so he could revive her? No. Lady Marigold wore breeches, smeared her face with coal dust, insisted on breaking into houses and morgues in the middle of the night and generally made his life much too taxing for his peace of mind.

Continuing to hold her in his arms, he was grateful to see they were already on his block. He could certainly not return her home passed out and dressed in breeches. As improper as it was for him to be bringing her to his bachelor home, given the circumstances of them fleeing the scene of a murder in a home they'd broken into, this was a minor offense.

Jonathan climbed out of the carriage and the driver proceeded to the back door and opened it, stepping aside so Jonathan could enter with his burden. "Thank you, John. Find your bed. I will see that Lady Marigold gets home."

How he planned to do that was questionable, but right now his main problem was getting her to wake up. He passed the kitchen and scullery, and continued to his drawing room, where he placed Marigold gently on a settee.

She began to move and moan. Then her eyes fluttered open, and she touched her hand to the back of her head. "Ouch. What happened?"

"Did you hit your head?" No wonder it had

taken her so long to awaken.

"Yes, I must have because it hurts. Ouch." She dropped her hand and suddenly sat up, grabbing the edge of the settee. "Oh, I don't think I should have done that."

"Lie back down and I'll get a cold cloth for your head." He headed to the doorway.

"What happened to the dead body?"

Jonathan snorted. "I didn't remain long enough to find out." He left the room and hunted down some clean cloths in the kitchen and dunked it into a pan of cool water.

When he returned to the drawing room, Marigold was sitting up, but still swaying a bit. "Honey, I think you should lie back down."

"I have to go home."

"Yes. I know you have to go home, but right now I need to check your head." He sat alongside where she'd laid back down on the settee. He felt around the back of her head and encountered a large bump. "Oh, yes. You did bang you head when you swooned."

"I don't swoon."

He grinned at her as he placed the cloth on her head. "Oh, no? What was it then?"

"I merely tripped on the dead body and fell, hit my head, and it appeared I had swooned." She winced when he placed the cloth on her head. "Ouch. Here, let me do it." She took the cloth from his hand and placed it gently on her head.

"I am going to have a brandy, but with a head injury, I don't think it would be a good idea for you to have one."

"Nonsense. I need a brandy as much as you. I

was the one who discovered the dead body."

He walked to the sidebar and poured a few fingers into his glass and less than one finger into Marigold's.

She took it from his hand and sipped. "What do we do now?"

"Nothing." He shook his head. "The last thing we want to do is get involved with a murder."

Marigold took another sip of her brandy. "Do you believe there is a connection between the man who sold the journal and ended up dead, then the man we assumed stole it from him and also ended up dead?"

"As I've said before. I do not believe in coincidences."

"The question now is, was he killed for the journal? And if so, for what reason? We assumed St. Clair was killed for the journal because Dr. Paglia's partner wanted it for whatever reason. Most likely to see what Paglia had to say in his journal about what they worked on together. But as far as we know there was no third person, so why was it stolen again?"

Jonathan ran his fingers thorough is hair. "We have no certainty that the journal was stolen again. We didn't have enough time to do a thorough search. In fact, I have reached the point where I no longer want the journal. In fact, I wish I had never heard of it."

Marigold's jaw dropped. "No. What do you mean you don't want the journal? I'm not giving up on this. I think we have an even more important reason to discover what is going on."

"Why? It's obvious there is something wrong and sinister about that journal."

"Oh, don't be a ninnyhammer. We have been given a golden opportunity to solve a crime, and you wish to walk away from it." She plunked her empty glass on the table. "Well, I'm not. I intend to find out what happened and why."

Jonathan stood, prowled toward her and pulled her up by both her hands. "You. Will. Not." Then, for lack of a better idea, he pulled her against him and covered her lips with his.

***

Marigold melted against him. The pounding in her head turned into throbbing throughout her entire body. Lord Stanley knew how to kiss. No gentleman who had ever kissed her in a dark garden had affected her like this. His tongue nudged her lips, and he swept in, sending shivers of desire straight to her core.

He cupped her cheeks and angled her head, so he could take the kiss deeper, his lips hard and searching. Just as she realized she'd stopped breathing, he pulled back and scattered kisses over her face, light butterfly kisses. "Damn, you drive me crazy. I want to throttle you and bed you at the same time."

She yanked his cravat lose and tossed it on the floor, then returned the scattered kisses he'd given her to his warm throat. "I prefer bedding to throttling."

"Don't say that." He sucked on her ear lobe, his hand wandering up her body until he cupped her breast, releasing a slight moan.

Marigold yanked his shirt free of his trousers and slid her hands up his warm torso. He shivered, gooseflesh popping up on his skin as she ran her palm over his muscles. "Why shouldn't I say that?"

"Because I am very close to scooping you up and taking you to my bedchamber."

She nibbled on his neck and soothed it with her tongue. "I've always wondered what a gentleman's bedchamber looked like."

He fisted her hair and pulled her head back, his face hovering over hers. His eyes were dark, brooding, intense. She could almost see the steam coming off his heated body. "I have wanted you for so long, months before we even got involved in this journal. I just didn't recognize it. I thought I disliked you, when actually I was fighting the strong attraction."

"Why fight?" She fumbled with the buttons on his trouser flap.

He covered her hand with his. "Are you absolutely sure this is what you want, Marigold? Because if you say no, I will bundle you up into my carriage and bring you home. You are playing with fire."

"I've always been on the dangerous side."

"I know." He bent and lifted her into his arms. "While I have always taken the safe road." He kissed her and started toward the stairs. "But no more, sweetheart. No more."

He kicked the door to his bedchamber open, strode across the room and dropped her in the middle of the bed. She giggled as she bounced several times.

The room was dark, with scant moonlight filtering through the window. She could not see much of the room, only make out shadows of furniture. Jonathan bent and lit a candelabra on the small table alongside the bed. "I want to see what I have been dreaming about for weeks."

Marigold sat up and climbed to her knees. "Me, too."

He knelt next to her. "You have been dreaming, as well?"

She reached up and touched his cheek. "Oh, yes."

That seemed to be all the encouragement he needed. With one swift movement, he had her shirt pulled from her breeches, and over her head. She did the same with him, until they were both free of their clothing.

He eased her back until she laid on the bed, her unbound hair spread out on the pillow. He sucked in a breath and just stared at her. "You are so beautiful, you take my breath away."

Her confidence faltered, and she moved to cover herself with her hands.

"No, you don't." He took her hands and laid them by her side. "I have waited for this moment for quite some time. Please let me look my fill."

After a few moments, he seemed to sense her unease, and laid next to her to pull her in for a deep kiss. That helped to rekindle her passion, and she returned his kiss with a fervor that matched his.

His hands swept her body, dipping into her curves, kneading the flesh of her breasts. She grew damp between her legs and felt a tightening in her stomach. Jonathan placed his mouth on one of her breasts and suckled, increasing the wonderful feelings.

Not one to be passive, she lightly drew her fingers over his manhood. He sucked in a breath, and she squeezed harder. "Yes, sweetheart. That feels good. The only problem is this won't last very long if you continue to do that."

She had no idea how wonderful the feelings were once a man was touching your naked skin. And she touching his. Her breasts felt heavy, and the moisture between her legs increased. In her study of anatomy, she knew very well what was happening to her body. Passion. Desire.

His fingers made his way to the area between her legs, flicking, touching, circling her moisture. She shifted her legs, feeling restless, needing something more. "That's it, sweetheart, come for me."

Although not completely sure what he meant, she knew there was something else that would increase the feelings she had. She pressed against his fingers and felt a slight jolt. "More."

"Yes, honey. Hang on. Don't push, let me do the work."

Her breathing increased, sweat broke out on her body, and all her attention was focused on the part of her body that Jonathan worked so diligently. After a few moments of licking her dry lips and tightening the muscles in her legs, she felt an explosion within her body like nothing she'd ever felt before. A rather loud moan escaped her, and she pushed hard against his hand, riding the wave of pleasure.

Once she slumped into the mattress, feeling absolutely boneless, Jonathan used his knee to widen her thighs and climbed between them, his hips fitted against hers. "This may hurt at first, but I promise it will only be for a second."

She knew about her maidenhead, and how breaking the barrier could hurt, but she wanted to feel him inside her so much, it mattered not. As he began to ease himself into her, she pushed up and he slid all the way in, his jaw tight as he stared at her, a slight smile pursing his lips. The books were right, the slight pinch only lasted a few seconds and then the fullness felt good.

Jonathan slid in and out of her body, as he held her head with his hands and kissed her. His movements grew frantic as she moved with him. "Sweetheart, I'm sorry, but I can't hold out any longer." After a few more thrusts, he shoved one last time, then pulled out of her, spilling his seed on her belly.

She played with his damp hair as he rested his head on her shoulder, them both breathing deeply, her heart pounding in rhythm next to his.

Yes, an affair would be quite the thing.

CHAPTER FOURTEEN

Jonathan awoke with a jerk. Something warm and soft was cuddled in front of him.

Marigold!

He quickly checked the china clock on the table next to his bed where the candles in the candelabra had burned almost completely down. Five o'clock in the morning.

He shook her shoulder, but she burrowed deeper into the covers. "Sweetheart, you have to wake up. I need to get you home. It will be light soon."

"No. I'm too tired, and I'm nice and warm."

Panic hit him at the thought of her being caught leaving his house at this hour. They had to get her home and inside her house within the next half hour, or daylight would arrive and the chances of her being spotted would increase.

"No. Up you go." He tossed the covers off and she yelped as the cold air hit her naked body.

She scrambled to pull the covers back, but he held them away from the bed. "No. Listen to me,

Marigold. It is five o'clock in the morning. You must get home before someone sees you leave here and return home."

She peeked at him through strands of her hair. "Five o'clock?"

"Yes."

As if shot from a cannon, she was up and pulling on her clothes. "Hurry. Get dressed."

Jonathan yawned and pulled on his clothes, fumbling in the dark. Within minutes they were clothed and downstairs. "I don't want to take time to ready the carriage, so since you're wearing breeches anyway, we will take my horse. If anyone does spot us, it will look like two men on the horse."

They made their way to the mews where the groom on duty quickly tacked his horse, and they were on their way. "I'm taking you to the back door."

Marigold shivered. The morning air was chilly, but he was sweating with his fear of the retribution for her if she was caught. Not only would they be forced to marry, which was something he'd decided halfway through their tupping, anyway, but it would take years for her reputation to recover, and he did not want to start off his marriage with a baroness under a cloud of scandal.

He would not relax until she was behind closed doors. He never should have fallen asleep after they'd had sex. It was so unusually odd for him to do, that he was still amazed.

Truth be told, as a gentleman, all his encounters until now had been with mistresses and the occasional lonely widow, but he'd always felt energized afterward and anxious to leave their bed and resume his day, or night.

Lying with Marigold had been so different. It had seemed perfectly normal to cozy up to her once they finished, and then found himself awakening from a deep, contented sleep. "We must have a serious discussion."

Marigold nodded. "I agree. We have to figure out how we are going to proceed with our investigation to find the journal and uncover the murderer."

"That is not what I mean, but we will discuss that, as well." They had arrived at her house, and he quickly went to the mews behind the row of townhouses. It was still dark but beginning to lighten as the sun started its ascent for the day.

He hopped off the horse and lifted her down. "I will see you to your door."

Heads down, hoping if they were spotted an observer would assume they were servants, he shuffled her through the garden and to the back door. He kissed her lightly on the lips. "Go now. I will call on you this afternoon."

Stifling a yawn, she nodded, opened the door and disappeared.

Now that she was safely in her house, fatigue hit him, and he scrubbed his face with his hands. What he needed now was several hours of sleep. He would call on Marigold this afternoon, explain the situation to her, and then ask to speak with Lord Pomeroy.

He was a bit concerned about how she thought they would continue with trying to find the journal. At this point it had all become much too dangerous.

It was on the ride home that he remembered Mr. Townsend, a friend of his from Eton. He'd been born on the wrong side of the blanket, but his father, the Viscount Latham had paid for him to have a decent education. He was a friendly sort, always willing to help, which is what made him accepted at school. At least no more unaccepted than any of the other boys were.

School was sometimes a difficult place to be since most of the teachers turned their attention away from scuffling among their students, with the excuse that they needed to learn how to handle themselves.

Townsend had taken a position with Scotland Yard after time spent in His Majesty's Service. He told Jonathan that after Boney's defeat, military life had not appealed to him. With his father's permission, he sold his commission and decided law enforcement was his forte.

To soothe Marigold's quest for justice, he would speak with Townsend at his club later in the day to find out whatever information was available about the murder. With any luck, his former schoolmate might even be willing to keep him abreast of the investigation.

Hopefully that would satisfy Marigold and keep her out of further trouble.

***

Marigold closed the back door of her home, and quietly made her way down the corridor, past the servants' quarters. They would be stirring soon to begin preparing the house for the day. She went up the back stairway and lightly tread to her room, avoiding the known creaky boards. Breathing a sigh of relief, she entered her room.

And looked straight into Lady Crampton's eyes.

Shock almost had her swooning again until she

remembered she did not swoon. She closed the door and took in a deep breath. Lady Crampton was clothed in her nightgown and dressing robe and sat on Marigold's bed, her arms crossed. "Good morning, Lady Marigold."

Marigold licked her suddenly dry lips, her heart pounding and her stomach roiling almost enough to bring up her stomach contents. "I can explain."

"Please do."

Before she started she had to know if the worse had happened. "Does Papa know?"

"No. Or should I say not yet."

Marigold nodded, understanding she was very close to disaster. "It's a long story, and I am quite fatigued. Is it possible we can have this conversation later?"

Lady Crampton's brows rose. "And give you time to make up some sort of story you think I am foolish enough to believe? I think not."

Marigold nodded again and ran her sweaty palms down her legs. "I didn't think so."

"Before you start, I want you to understand I am so very relieved to see you. I had been afraid you and Lord Stanley had eloped, which would have destroyed your father. However, I am not mistaken that this little adventure of yours tonight included his lordship?"

Another nod.

"You may begin." Lady Crampton scooted over on the bed and patted the space alongside her. "Sit. You look quite pale, my dear. If I didn't know better, I would think you were about to swoon."

"I don't swoon."

"So you've said many times before." She waved

her arm. "Continue."

"You see, it all started with a journal." Marigold continued with her story, leaving out the part where they visited the morgue, which she was afraid would cause Lady Crampton a complete collapse, but was forced to mention Dr. Stevenson since she had to explain where she was tonight.

"You broke into someone's house and found a dead body!" Lady Crampton's face grew pale and her breathing increased. Perhaps she should have left that part of the story out, too. Except then she would not have any story to tell, and she didn't think her chaperone would believe she and Jonathan were out strolling Hyde Park.

"Yes, we did," she hurried on before Lady Crampton could escape her room and summon her father. "But no one saw us. I am sure the police will be notified, and they will investigate the matter."

Apparently stunned into silence, Lady Crampton continued to stare at her. After a few minutes of Marigold fidgeting, waiting for her to speak, she said, "I must say, Marigold, I have no words. In fact, I need to digest what you've told me after I've had some sleep."

She stood and hugged her. "You need some sleep as well." With those few words, she headed to the door, shaking her head.

"Lady Crampton?"

She turned, her hand on the latch. "Yes, dear."

"Will you tell Papa?"

"I do not wish to be the cause of his sudden death." She left the room, closing the door silently as she departed.

Marigold sighed and removed her clothes. She

would love a bath but didn't want to summon the household staff so early with all the other duties they had. Giving her hands and face a quick wash, she pulled on her nightgown, crawled into bed and was fast asleep almost before her head hit the pillow.

The expected summons came later in the afternoon. Marigold had slept well past noon, had a bath, a breakfast tray in her room, and spent the rest of the time sitting on the window box seat in her bedchamber, pretending to read a book, but actually relieving the night before.

She was no longer a maiden. The thought both thrilled and frightened her. But now that the deed had been done, perhaps Jonathan would be more receptive to an affair. She was a woman of the world, after all. She felt no need to saddle herself with a husband.

As she made her way downstairs, her bravado took a flight at the thought of facing Papa. But instead of him waiting for her in the library, the footman directed her to the drawing room where Jonathan awaited her. She breathed a sigh of relief as she entered the room. "Oh, it's only you."

His brows rose to his hairline. "That is quite a nebulous greeting."

"Oh, my apologies." She took a seat on the edge of the settee. "I see tea has already been ordered."

"Yes. I visited with Lady Crampton for a little bit before she sent for you to join me. This one is a replacement for the one we just finished."

"Oh, dear." Perhaps this visit would not be so pleasant after all. "What did you speak of?" She tried to show her indifference by pouring tea for the two of them, but her shaky hand gave her away.

"Apparently, you are aware that she knows where you were last night."

Marigold snorted. "Since I was the one who told her—after finding her waiting for me in my bedchamber—I am fully aware of what she knows."

Jonathan accepted the cup of tea from her hand. "Now that she is apprised of the situation, continuing in this matter must now come to an end."

"I don't agree."

"I didn't think you would. However, Lady Crampton is no one to fool with. She told me if I allowed you to continue in this situation, she would advise your father about our escapade last night."

"You mean she hasn't told him?" Even though her chaperone had made the statement about not causing her papa's sudden death, Marigold really didn't think she wouldn't tell him.

"No. And for that you should be most grateful."

"Indeed, I am very grateful." She shifted in her seat and asked eagerly, "What will you do from here?"

"I have a friend in the Bow Street Runners, Mr. Townsend. I think he might be willing to help in an informal sort of way."

"Oh, how wonderful to have a friend there. When do you plan to visit with Mr. Townsend?"

"Soon." He took a sip of tea, and then sat back. "But before we delve into that, I wish to discuss something with you."

She couldn't imagine what would be more important that visiting with the man from Scotland Yard and getting information on the murder. "Go on."

"I have decided it is time to marry."

Botheration! Just as she was ready to commit to

an affair, he decided to up and marry and leave her. "Well, that is annoying. Who is the unfortunate lady?"

Jonathan choked on his tea and stared at her in disbelief. "You!"

CHAPTER FIFTEEN

Jonathan placed his teacup in the saucer. "Marigold, why would I propose marriage to anyone else? We have been intimate. You might be carrying my child."

Marigold chewed her lip. "I was afraid you were going to say that. However, in my studies in anatomy, I know how children are conceived. You withdrew, so your seed did not enter me. Therefore, it is highly unlikely I am pregnant."

Jonathan scrubbed his face with his hands. "You say the most outrageous things. No gently reared young lady should know about that. Or speak of it. It is not done."

"Neither is lying with a man one is not married to, but we did it. Did we not?"

He groaned and hopped up. He paced for a minute, running his fingers through his hair. "Yes. We did. That is precisely why we must marry. If word got out, if anyone saw you leave my house, if anyone saw me escort you to your back door, you would be ruined."

The mulish expression on her face told him an argument was about to ensue, but before she could say a word, the butler entered the room. "My lord. Your presence is requested in the library. Lord Pomeroy awaits you."

Lord Pomeroy awaits you.

His stomach dropped to his feet and he broke into a sweat. Lady Crampton said she would not tell Lord Pomeroy if Marigold ceased her investigatory activities. But, nevertheless, Jonathan had a feeling his lordship had not requested his presence so they could share a brandy again.

"Very well." He turned to Marigold. "Do not leave the house. This conversation is not finished."

She drew herself up and he knew immediately he had said the wrong thing. Lady Marigold Smith was not the sort of woman one ordered about. Before she could give him a good lashing with her tongue, he bowed and made a quick exit behind the butler.

Lord Pomeroy appeared as pleasant as he had the last time the two of them had shared a brandy. Except this time tea service had been set out. Jonathan's visit had certainly kept the kitchen busy. Visits with three household members, three tea services. He would most likely float out of the house.

"You wished to speak with me, my lord?"

Pomeroy waved at a seat in front of the tea service. "Yes, yes, my boy. Have a seat."

At least the man seemed far too cheerful to request Jonathan contact his second, so they could set up the day and time for the duel. Still uneasy at facing the man whose unmarried daughter he'd bedded the night before, he sat, and once again accepted a cup of tea, passed on the treats, and sat back waiting for what Pomeroy was about to say.

"I don't sleep well." Pomeroy took a sip of tea and regarded Jonathan over the top of the rim.

Uh, oh. This was not going to end well. "I am sorry to hear that, my lord."

"A curse, to be sure." He reached for one of the delicate sandwiches and made a face. "I used to complain because when my dear Elise ran my household, before she married St. George, she only offered these silly little sandwiches. Said it was better for my health." He popped one into his mouth. "I thought once she married I would be able to have something a bit hardier at tea time. Then the charming Lady Crampton came into our lives—as a chaperone for my precious daughters—" he hurried to add, leaving Jonathan wondering why the man seemed flustered in mentioning Lady Crampton, and her duties.

"Her idea of tea sandwiches wasn't much better." He waved at the table. "As you can see." Another delicate sandwich disappeared into Pomeroy's mouth. "Where was I?" He wiped his mouth with a napkin. "Oh, yes. My trouble sleeping."

Jonathan tensed.

"Wouldn't you know I woke up right before daylight this morning and found it necessary to take a stroll to the kitchen for a glass of warm milk. Wasn't really looking for more sleep time, just a way to fill the belly a bit before Cook would have something ready for my breakfast."

Jonathan was not stupid and knew exactly where this conversation was headed. Should he play dumb and wait for Pomeroy to confront him, or offer his sincere apologies and state his full intention to marry

Marigold?

"If one wanders the house at night—or in this case early morning—it's an easy way to keep track of one's family members' comings and goings. Caught my lovely daughter, Juliet, Lady Hertford that is, and her husband tiptoeing down the corridor to the back door one time a few years ago in the middle of the night." He picked up another sandwich and studied it before popping it into his mouth. "They weren't married yet."

Since Pomeroy's ramblings had not wandered in the direction of a question, Jonathan kept his mouth shut.

With one quick move, the man sat forward on his seat and glared at Jonathan. "So, since my wandering this morning was interrupted by my cherished daughter—dressed in breeches—tiptoeing down the corridor from the back door before six this morning, and not being a fool, I know it had something to do with you. When can I expect an offer?"

No point in continuing to play dumb. Lord Pomeroy was not.

"In fact, my lord, I have suggested such to Lady Marigold already this morning."

"But not a formal proposal? If I recall, I asked you to come to me first."

"No. Not an actual, formal proposal. But in any event, she does not seem amenable to the idea."

Pomeroy waved. He was either dismissing his comments or shooing away the annoying fly who had been bothering them since they'd sat down. "No matter. She will. Eventually."

Apparently satisfied with Jonathan's answer,

Pomeroy leaned back once again, his legs stretched out and crossed at the ankles, his fingers laced on his stomach. "We have a sort of family tradition here. The whole family gathers when a marriage proposal is made."

Once again, Jonathan choked on his tea.

***

Marigold paced her bedroom, pushed her spectacles back up on her nose, and counted the flowers on her carpet as she walked, mentally dividing them into squares against the length and width of the rug, and concluded the carpet was out of balance. At least it had helped somewhat to not dwell completely on how thoroughly annoyed she'd been that Jonathan had gotten to speak with his friend, Mr. Townsend from Scotland Yard to discuss the Stevenson murder, and she'd been denied. Thwarted on two counts, she'd been.

If she insisted on visiting with Townsend when Jonathan did, he would tell Lady Crampton, who would tell Papa about her disgrace. Aside from that, women were never allowed in men's clubs, so she couldn't have gone anyway. Blast all men. They controlled everything, and that annoyed her even more than being shut out of the investigation.

She did vaguely suggest to Jonathan that she dress as a man and go with him, but for once in her life she didn't pursue that argument. The look on his face was enough to stifle any discussion. She might be clever and daring, but she wasn't stupid.

Another concern was Papa's request to visit with Jonathan. She'd watched from her bedchamber window and saw Jonathan leave about twenty minutes before. He looked whole and hardy, so there apparently hadn't been fisticuffs, although Jonathan said Lady Crampton would not tell Papa about her adventure as long as she stayed out of the investigation.

However, Jonathan had ordered her to stay in the house, so they could continue their conversation. Apparently, he did not think the issue was so very important, after all since he had strolled away without looking back.

A scratch at her bedchamber door drew her attention. "Come."

The door opened and her two sisters, Juliet, the Marchioness Hertford, and Elise, the Countess St. George, strolled into her room.

Marigold broke out into a huge smile. "What are you both doing here? Are the little ones with you?"

"Of course. They are happily settled in the nursery, eating biscuits when we left," Elise said. Then she opened her arms. "Come give me a hug."

The three sisters gathered in a circle as they did when they were younger and hugged each other. "I'm so glad you came to visit," Marigold said, hating the tears she fought to keep back. It was truly so very good to be with her sisters again. So much had happened since the last time they were all together.

Elise sat on the settee by the window and smoothed her skirts. "We were summoned."

"Summoned? By whom?"

"Papa," Juliet said as she joined Elise on the settee. "He is planning some sort of a special dinner this evening. He said there would be entertainment."

"Entertainment?" Whatever could Papa have

been talking about? At least since he hadn't yet learned about her debacle, it would not involve any sort of repute of her with the family all watching. "Are St. George and Hertford with you?"

Elise patted the open seat next to her for Marigold to sit. "St. George will be here later. He had parliamentary business to attend to."

"Hertford is expected momentarily. I believe Papa wanted advice on an investment." Juliet shrugged. "Those things are all beyond me."

Elise viewed Marigold with the look she'd bestowed on her and Juliet when Elise had taken over Mother's duties after she passed away. "Are you telling me that you have no idea what Papa is planning in the way of entertainment?"

Marigold shook her head. "No." She hesitated and then added. "I've been busy of late with a matter that needed my attention."

She never should have said a word because both Elise and Juliet perked up with a great deal more enthusiasm than Marigold would have liked.

"Tell us." Juliet was practically jumping up and down on the settee. "With our boring lives, we have so little to gossip about."

"Nonsense. I'm sure the children and all the *ton* gossip keep you both very well diverted."

"Actually, Hertford and I haven't been to many social events this Season." Juliet blushed prettily. "We are, um, expecting another little one in several months. And you know how over-protective my husband is when I am increasing."

"Juliet! How wonderful." Marigold and Elise both hugged her.

"Well, since announcements are being made, I

should add that St. George and I will be adding to our nursery in a few months, as well." Elise grinned at her two sisters.

"My goodness. The family is certainly growing." Marigold placed her hand on her stomach, hoping she would not be adding to the numbers.

Of course, both of her sisters noticed her movement. Elise raised a brow and nudged Juliet. "Are you certain you have no idea what Papa is all about tonight, dear youngest sister?"

Marigold shook her head. "No. I have no idea."

"Mari, why don't you freshen up and join us downstairs? We will take all the children on a walk. It will do us good since the air is so very fresh today."

Marigold smiled at her sister. "You haven't called me that in years. I do agree that a walk is a wonderful idea. I will join you in a few minutes."

Elise and Juliet left the room, arm in arm. "We will gather the children and their nurses and see you downstairs," Elise tossed over her shoulder.

While she washed her face and hands and re-did her hairdo, Marigold's thoughts wandered back to the situation with Jonathan and his proposal. Not that it had been a proper proposal, and truth be known, even though she had considered suggesting an affair, she knew deep down he would never consent to that. He was too much of a gentleman. And, he needed an heir.

Even if she didn't want to marry, she could never tolerate being Jonathan's lover and have him marry someone else. In fact, if she was being totally truthful, she would not be too happy to see him wed another, even if they weren't lovers.

Now that was a scary thought. Jealous? She

refused to believe that, but what else could explain the stabbing sensation to her heart when she imagined Jonathan marrying one of those silly girls from the marriage mart?

Because I love him.

Air whooshed from her lungs. She had to sit down for that one, or she would surely swoon. And she didn't swoon.

CHAPTER SIXTEEN

Jonathan arrived at the Pomeroy townhouse after having bathed, shaved, and dressed appropriately for dinner. He chuckled to himself at what Lord Pomeroy had planned. The man was almost as slick and devious as his daughter. It was nice to have him on his side.

He patted the piece of jewelry in his pocket and smiled at Macon as he held the front door open for him. "Good evening, my lord. If you will follow me to the drawing room, Lady Marigold has asked that you join her there before the others gather for dinner."

Not long after Jonathan was settled in a comfortable chair in front of the fireplace, Marigold swept into the room. A fine pale blue material flowed over the dark blue underskirt of her gown. Slight capped sleeves covered the very top of her slender arms. A gold woven piece of fabric circled her body under her luscious breasts, with another of the same trim edging the neckline of her gown. Gold slippers peeked from under the bottom of her skirts.

Her glorious hair had been swept from her face, held back with two jeweled combs, with a mass of curls tumbling down her back. Even her spectacles seemed to glimmer in the candlelight. She smiled at him.

He slowly stood, his breath hitched, and as if he'd been struck by a thunderbolt, the thought jumped to the front of his mind.

I love her.

How could he have been so blind to the fact? That was why he wanted to marry her. Not just because it was his duty to produce an heir, or his responsibility to the girl because he'd compromised her. He wanted her because his life would be empty without her. She was daring, frustrating, always on the edge of disaster, but she was also intelligent, kind, witty, and caring.

She would make a wonderful baroness.

Her smiled faltered as he continued to stare at her. "Is something wrong?"

He crossed the room, shaking his head. "Not at all, I am merely taken aback at your beauty."

Expecting a bit of sarcasm, he was surprised when she executed a perfect curtsy. "Thank you, my lord. You are looking exceptionally handsome yourself tonight."

Unable to help himself, he took both her hands and pulled her to him. Wrapping his arms around her, he bent his head and took her lips in a warm, loving kiss. As much as he wanted to toss her on the sofa next to him and have his way with her, want he really wanted, was to show her by his kiss how much he cared for her.

Before she decorated him with the contents of her dinner plate at the dining table when she learned what he intended to do.

He pulled back but kept his arms around her waist. "I have news about the murder investigation."

"You do? Tell me."

Jonathan took her by the hand and led her to the sofa. Once they were settled, he leaned back and rested his foot on his bent knee. "I saw Mr. Townsend today, for a brief period at his club. The investigation is moving quite quickly. It seems that Dr. Vincenzio Paglia had a nephew from whom he was estranged. The man's name is Mr. Giovanni Paglia.

"The reason his name was readily available was because he had already been under investigation for Dr. Vincenzio Paglia's death. They were almost certain he had murdered his uncle but had been unable to prove it."

"Oh, my goodness. Do you suppose he killed St. Clair and Stevenson? Do you think it was because of the journal?"

"I don't know. I told Townsend about the journal and he was going to add that information to the file. Although they were still counting St. Clair's death as an accident, the young Paglia is on their books for Dr. Stevenson's murder."

"Where does that leave our journal?"

"Missing." He laughed. "But, Townsend assured me when they find it, wherever it might be, the journal will be returned. To me."

"To us."

"Perhaps." He grinned. Yes. Most likely it would be to them both.

"Here you two are. Why don't you join the rest of us in the library where Lord Pomeroy is handing out glasses of brandy and sherry?" Lady Crampton stuck her head into the room, a bright smile on her face.

"Yes. Of course." Jonathan offered his arm to Marigold and they strolled, along with Lady Crampton to the library.

Jonathan knew Hertford and St. George but had not spent time in their company since their marriages. They nodded to each other, and he bowed to their wives.

He took a glass of brandy from Lord Pomeroy, and brought a glass of sherry to Marigold, who was busy chatting with her sisters and Lady Crampton. He was quite surprised when two very pretty young ladies, identical twins if he was not mistaken, joined them in the library.

Lady Crampton's brought them over to Jonathan. "My lord, may I make known to you my daughters, Lady Prudence and Lady Phoebe." She smiled at the two young ladies. "Girls, this is The Right Honorable Lord Stanley."

Both girls offered an excellent curtsy.

"It is a pleasure to meet you, ladies. I had no idea Lady Crampton hid such loveliness from the rest of the world." He turned to Lady Crampton and grinned. "Not well done, my lady."

Both girls collapsed into giggles, a bright blush rising to their cheeks. They appeared to be about three and ten years.

"We have been studying deBretts. I believe you are a baron, my lord. Is that correct?" One of the girls, he had no idea which one, smiled at him.

"Yes, indeed. I am a baron."

Lord Pomeroy moved to the center of the room. "Now that we are all gathered here together, I will ask that everyone take a seat."

Jonathan took Marigold's elbow and escorted her to the settee. He ran his finger around the inside of his cravat and waited until everyone was settled. Then taking a deep breath, he went down on one knee.

***

Marigold's eyes swung from person to person and realized they had all been watching her since they'd entered the room. Her sisters were smiling at her, dabbing their eyes with lace handkerchiefs. Lady Prudence and Lady Phoebe were practically bouncing on the sofa.

Once she settled on the settee and Jonathan dropped to one knee, Marigold hopped up. "Papa!" Her gaze swung to him, her lips tightening.

Lord Pomeroy gazed lovingly at her from across the room. "Yes, my dear heart."

"Papa, no."

He shook his head. "Papa, yes, darling girl. 'Tis a family tradition."

Marigold sat back on the settee and dropped her head into her hands. "This is so very embarrassing."

"How do you think I feel?" Jonathan offered from his place on the floor as he ran his finger around the inside of his cravat again.

Marigold picked up her head and looked at him. This was the man she loved. He was bossy, over-protective and arrogant at times. He was also loving, caring, intelligent and fun to be with. He would also allow her the freedom she must absolutely have for the rest of her life.

"Within reason, Marigold."

To her horror, she realized she'd been mumbling out loud. Fortunately, no one heard her except Jonathan.

He took her hand and looked up at her. "Marigold, there isn't a lot I can say, except I love you, and hope you will make me the happiest of men and accept my hand in marriage."

She closed her eyes briefly, then looked at him. "I love you, too, Jonathan. And yes, I will marry you."

Cheers rose from the others in the room. This so-called tradition of every proposal having to be made in front of the entire family was growing tiresome. Except now hers was over, so it would all end until it was Prudence or Phoebe's turn.

Which led her to another heart stabbing thought. With her married, there would be no reason for Lady Crampton to continue living at their house and acting as chaperone. Whatever would happen to the girls? Where would they all go?

Before that line of thinking continued, Jonathan placed a heavy ring on her finger. It was a large ruby surrounded by tiny diamonds.

"This was my mother's ring. If you wish to have it re-set, please let me know."

Marigold shook her head and held out her hand to admire the ring on her finger. "No. I love it just the way it is. And I love that it was your mother's."

He climbed to his feet and pulled her up. Lord Pomeroy raised his glass. "As sad as I am at losing my treasured youngest daughter, I wish you happy."

The others stood and raised their glasses and

offered their best wishes. As if on cue—maybe it actually was—Macon entered the library to announce dinner. They all trooped into the dining room, ignoring precedence, and seated themselves at the table.

Once the soup course had been served, Marigold leaned toward Jonathan. "I am sorry you had to stumble into my family's unusual tradition of family proposals."

He covered her hand with his. "Not as long as it came to a successful end."

"It would be hard to say no with everyone watching."

Jonathan viewed her with narrowed eyes. "You weren't about to say 'no' were you?"

She took a sip of wine and grinned. Let him worry about that.

Three days later, Marigold managed to escape the house and Lady Crampton's chasing her with lists for the wedding things that needed to be done. She and Jonathan were taking a ride to Hyde Park. They hadn't attended any events since their betrothal, although an announcement had been sent to the newspaper.

He helped her into his phaeton and then circled the vehicle to climb up and take up the ribbons. "I think the weather should hold out until we finish at least one circle around the park." He glanced up at the cloudy sky.

"I am just grateful to be out of the house. Lady Crampton has so many lists, she has a list to keep track of her lists." She shook her head. "Don't get me wrong, I am very grateful for her arranging the wedding, since I have no idea what to do."

"Well, just sit back and enjoy the ride."

"Have you heard anything from Mr. Townsend?"

"Nothing. I don't want to insert myself too much because he does have a job to do. I'm sure if something important happened in the case, he would notify me."

It was apparent from the moment they entered the park that their betrothal was the current on *dit* for the *ton*. Gentlemen who had always flocked to her side cast unfriendly glances at Jonathan, and the young girls and their mothers who had hoped to catch a wealthy and handsome titled gentleman offered best wishes to them, the sweetness dripping from their lips, and the snarls and scowls back in place once they passed by.

It was all rather comical, actually.

"Oh, dear. I believe it's beginning to rain." Marigold raised her hand, palm up, as two drops of water splashed on her hand.

Jonathan glanced up. "Yes. You are right. I am afraid our ride has ended. I will head toward your house."

Marigold touched his hand with hers. "No. Please. Can we not proceed to your house, instead? I'm afraid Lady Crampton will have another task for me, or another list to go over."

Jonathan shrugged. "Since we are betrothed, I am sure it is no problem for you to visit my house for a short while."

"Thank you." Marigold leaned back and took a deep breath, happy to have escaped being picked and prodded by the dressmaker who had moved into their servants' wing, or made to check off items on one of Lady Crampton's many lists.

They managed to get to Jonathan's house before the deluge began and were in his drawing room with tea and biscuits for about ten minutes when his butler Coombs appeared at the drawing room door. He was pale, and sweating. "My lord, you have a guest."

Jonathan stood as the butler came farther into the room. A man walked behind him, two pistols pushed against the servant's back.

"Lord Stanley, I presume?" the man said.

When Jonathan nodded, the man immediately turned and conked Coombs on the head. Coombs fell like a rock. The interloper grinned, his white teeth like a wolf waiting to attack its prey. Although he held two menacingly looking pistols, he bowed as if they were meeting in a ballroom. "I am Mr. Giovanni Paglia."

CHAPTER SEVENTEEN

Jonathan's first thought was getting Marigold out of the room, and out of the house. A man with a pistol was a dangerous matter, with two pistols and Marigold's tendency to jump into things, disaster loomed. He was terrified she would attempt to disarm the man and end up dead.

That scared him more than the pistol pointed at his heart. "Unfortunately, given the circumstances, I cannot truthfully say it is a pleasure to meet you. I would send for tea, but I have the feeling you are not expecting the usual comforts when calling on a gentleman." He glanced at Coombs lying on the floor. "And my butler is currently not available to summon tea."

"While I appreciate you sense of humor, Lord Stanley, I am not here for tea, or even conversation."

Jonathan waved to a chair. "Why don't you sit, and we will discuss your visit. I just ask that Lady Marigold be allowed to leave the room." He ignored the gasp from her at his side. Blasted woman was probably busy planning her attack on the gunman.

"I think not, Lord Stanley. In fact, you and I and the young lady are all going to take a walk upstairs to the top floor of this house."

"And what interest have you in my nursery? It is not yet filled, you know." Perhaps light banter would give him time to think of a way to disarm the man without anyone being hurt.

"Move," Paglia growled.

No light banter, then. Jonathan would rush the man, but Marigold was a definite unknown. While she remained with them, he could do nothing reckless.

The three of them trotted up the stairs to the nursery. Thank goodness Marigold seemed to be in a somnolent state and just obeyed what the man demanded. Maybe he should employ this man's tactics when dealing with his betrothed in the future.

Once they entered the room that would one day be a nursery if he and Marigold were lucky enough to get out of this situation, Jonathan moved away from Marigold, keeping Paglia's attention on him. The two of them side-by-side was too much of an easy target. "You have apparently brought us up here with the idea of doing us harm. May I have the privilege of knowing why?"

"You read his journal."

"I assume you mean Dr. Vincenzio Paglia's journal?"

"That's right. I had to get it back before anyone read it." He grinned that feral grin again, while Jonathan's mind worked furiously to figure out how to get the two of them out of the mess they were in. "The old man wrote in it every day. I ransacked his house after he died, but it was nowhere to be found.

How St. Clair ended up with it is a mystery I have no time to concern myself with. All I want is to keep everything about Paglia nice and quiet."

"Is that why you killed St. Clair and Dr. Stevenson?"

Paglia waved one of the pistols causing Jonathan's heart to almost stop. "St. Clair was an idiot. If he had given me a straight answer at the start, I wouldn't have had to get into a tussle with him. A weak man. One good shove and he collapsed against the brick fireplace."

"Dr. Stevenson?"

"He was my uncle's partner. There was every reason to believe he would interfere with my plans, so he had to die."

"What is in the journal that you are so protective of?"

"You know. You read it."

Jonathan shook his head. "No. I never got the chance to read it. You stole it."

Marigold glanced at Jonathan, her brows raised.

It had come to him as they all stood there that he'd been right, and it was near impossible for Dr. Stevenson to have crawled through Jonathan's library window and stolen the journal. The poor man never had possession of the book. This man, Dr. Paglia's nephew, had stolen the journal from Jonathan.

"I don't believe you didn't read it." Paglia stared at them both. Jonathan was afraid this was it. If Paglia only had one pistol, he might take a chance, but if he rushed him with two pistols in his hands, Marigold might be shot.

"I have a rather generous contract with a publisher to publish my uncle's memoirs." Paglia shook his head and scowled at Jonathan's raised brows. "Not that blasted journal."

"Language, Mr. Paglia," Marigold offered.

"My apologies, my lady." He bowed, and Jonathan began to think this entire scene was a dream. If it were, he would love to wake up and find he and Marigold were safe.

"There are secrets in that journal that once revealed, would keep my publisher from following through on the contract. I need the money, you see."

So, there were records in the journal that probably involved ideas Paglia may have stolen from Dr. Stevenson. More than ever, Jonathan wanted his hands on the journal.

After he saved himself and Marigold from death.

Moving from foot to foot, and sweating profusely, it appeared Paglia was done with conversation.

Jonathan had to act now. "Marigold, do what you never do," he shouted.

Marigold dropped to the ground in a faint, and the quick movement startled Paglia, who looked in Marigold's direction. The second Marigold began to slump, Jonathan lunged forward, knocking one of the pistols out of Paglia's hand.

Paglia drew back his other hand, waving the gun. Jonathan lunged for the man's middle and took him to the floor where they rolled, both fighting for the gun.

"Jonathan, move away, I'll shoot him." Marigold held the pistol Jonathan had kicked away, waving it around. Bloody hell, the woman would probably shoot him, or herself in the foot.

"Leave the room, Marigold. Go for help."

Paglia was not the best pugilist, but he was small and wiry, and difficult to hang onto. The gun in his hand was a problem, also. Jonathan drew his arm back and plowed his fist into Paglia's face. Blood spurted from his nose, splattering over Jonathan's face.

The gun went off and Marigold screamed.

CHAPTER EIGHTEEN

Two weeks later

Marigold examined herself in the mirror, taking one last look before she left her bedchamber for the last time and became Jonathan's wife. Her cream-colored gown was the loveliest piece she'd ever owned. Small pale pink roses had been embroidered on the capped sleeves, the hem of the gown, and brim of her bonnet, to match the roses she would carry with her.

Her wedding day. There was a time when she thought this day would never arrive because she would be buried six feet under the ground.

Mr. Giovanni Paglia had been dragged moaning and cursing from Jonathan's house by members of the Metropolitan Police. He was now spending his time in Newgate while the investigation into the two murders proceeded. Mr. Townsend had assured Jonathan that *their* journal would be returned to them, hopefully within a few days.

But more importantly, by the end of this day, she

would be a married woman. Her hand rested on her middle where she suspected Jonathan's heir resided. She was still amazed that his seed was so strong she still ended up pregnant even though he had withdrawn the first time they lay together.

There had been a few more times they'd been able to sneak in some intimate time together, since betrothed couples were allowed a lot more leniency, but it had to have been the first time he'd bedded her for her courses to be missing.

Her thoughts returned to the day Mr. Paglia had held them both at gunpoint. She'd been scared to death that Jonathan had been shot when the gun went off and screamed enough to wake the dead. He, on the other hand, thought she had been shot and after knocking Mr. Paglia out cold with one good punch to the face, he'd jumped up and grabbed her.

They clung to each other until their breathing returned to normal. By then, several of the servants had arrived at the nursery door and soon Scotland Yard had been summoned and Paglia taken away.

The woman in her couldn't wait for the coming evening to be able to enjoy spending the entire night in Jonathan's arms. The curious scientist in her longed to be settled in bed with Jonathan at her side as they read the journal and discovered what was so important that Mr. Paglia murdered two people for it and was prepared to murder two more.

She and Jonathan had discussed the journal many times and had concluded that Dr. Paglia must have stolen some of Dr. Stevenson's ideas as his own work and had taken the credit for it.

"Marigold, come, we are all waiting for you." Elise slipped into the room with Juliet on her heels.

Both sisters glowed as they regarded her. Most likely from their pregnancies. Did she look the same?

"You look absolutely stunning, Mari." Elise dabbed at her eyes.

"Thank you." She hugged them both. "And I am ready." With one last look around her bedchamber, she left for her new life.

Jonathan waited for her at the front of the small chapel where they were to be wed. He followed her every move down the aisle, his face so full of love, she almost wept. But she did not weep. Nor did she swoon. Although that fake swoon certainly helped save their lives.

"You look beautiful, sweetheart." He reached for her hand and intertwined their fingers together as they turned to face the vicar who offered them a warm smile.

The vicar led them through the ceremony, saying all the official prayers, reciting the vows they needed to take. Marigold was not too happy about the 'love, honor and obey' part of the vows, but she wisely said nothing, although Jonathan did grin at her.

Blasted man.

Finally, they reached the end. The vicar blessed the ring she'd worn since her betrothal and handed it to Jonathan. He placed it onto her finger and declared, *"With this ring I thee wed, with my body I thee worship, and with all my worldly goods I thee endow. In the Name of the Father, and of the Son, and of the Holy Ghost. Amen."*

Of course, she wasn't weeping at those lovely words, but nevertheless she took the handkerchief he handed her and dabbed her eyes, tearful from the dust in the church.

The wedding breakfast that followed was quite a celebration. Champagne flowed, Papa gave several speeches, both her brothers-in-law teased Jonathan, and made comments she only heard part of, but knew they were the sort of remarks ladies tried very hard not to hear.

Soon her sisters accompanied her to Jonathan's house—which was her house now, also—where the new bride and groom would spend the night. They rushed her upstairs and stripped her, gave her another bath, and dressed her in the fine silk nightgown she'd had made especially for this night.

After more than an hour of lady-talk, Elise sat her on the edge of the bed and took her hand. "As I have been your mother since you were a young girl, I believe it is my duty to speak to you about what will happen tonight."

"Elise, I'm sure Lady Crampton already did that." Juliet turned to Marigold. "Did she not?"

Not wishing to let her sisters know she was already well prepared for the night's activities, having already practiced, and was anxious for them to leave so they could get started, she lied. "Of course. She spoke with me just this morning."

Elise sighed, most likely sad at having lost that part of her duties. Well, she had a daughter she could subject that lecture to. Instead, she held Marigold by her shoulders. "I can't believe my baby sister is married."

"Now don't you do this, Elise, or we will all be bawling like babes." Juliet grabbed a handkerchief from her reticule which she passed to her sisters. "This is a happy occasion and we should not be weeping."

"I don't weep." Marigold said as she blew her nose.

A light knock drew their attention. Jonathan opened the door, his hair damp from his bath. He held a bottle of champagne and two glasses. The sight of him in his red and blue striped banyan over his black trousers had Marigold licking her dry lips.

"It's time to leave ladies, I require time with my wife." He stared at Marigold the entire time he spoke. He seemed to have eyes for nothing and no one, but her.

She blushed under his perusal and wished her sisters far, far away.

He cast a glance at Elise and Juliet. "I have notified your driver that you will be leaving soon."

With a look passed between them and a slight smirk, Juliet and Elise hugged her one more time and departed. Jonathan closed the door and leaned against it. "You are the most beautiful bride who ever lived, Lady Stanley."

Marigold gave a slight dip. "Thank you, Lord Stanley. I believe you would hold the record for the handsomest bridegroom, as well."

***

An hour later, Jonathan climbed onto the bed, the journal in hand. They'd just finished a rousing bout of bedsport, and were now ready to read the journal that, for the most part, brought them together.

Mr. Townsend had arrived during the wedding breakfast and presented the book to Jonathan. Once invited to join the festivities, Townsend kept them laughing at the stories he told of various cases he had worked on. Jonathan was quite sure not all his cases were funny, but he wanted to entertain the ladies, not send them running to the chamber pot.

He poured two glasses of champagne and handed one to Marigold. Since the room was warm enough from the low fire that burned, neither had bothered to dress. They sat side by side, their warm flesh touching.

"Are you ready?" Jonathan asked.

Marigold's eyes burned with enthusiasm. "Yes. I can hardly wait."

They sipped their champagne, then Jonathan took the glasses and placed them on the table next to the bed. "We don't want to damage the book."

Snuggled together, he opened the first page. They leaned over to look at the writing in the illumination from the candelabra.

They read. Then read again. Jonathan frowned and glanced at his wife.

Marigold frowned.

He turned to another page and they read.

He flipped more pages.

They read more pages.

Finally, Jonathan slammed the book shut, and looked at Marigold. "Huh."

"Yes."

They sat for a moment, taking in what they'd just read.

"Correct me if I am wrong, my lord, but there was nothing on those pages except love letters."

"You are correct, my dear. Letters to his lover."

They looked at each other and both spoke at the same time. "His male lover."

"That was the secret Mr. Paglia wanted to keep

from being known. He knew his uncle's reputation would be ruined and the publisher would never publish his memoirs."

Marigold shrugged and took the journal out of his hand, tossing it over her shoulder. "I can think of better things to occupy our time."

"Indeed." He blew out the candles and they slid farther under the covers.

EPILOGUE

Lord Henry Pomeroy settled into the most comfortable chair in his library, a glass of brandy in one hand, the latest book he'd been reading in the other. With all the nonsense surrounding his youngest daughter, Marigold's wedding, he'd had little time to relax with his favorite things to do. Read and drink a brandy.

The only thing missing was Selina, Lady Crampton, the woman who acted as chaperone and companion to his two younger daughters before they married. Generally, she joined him in the evenings when she wasn't accompanying Marigold to an event. She would sit and work on her embroidery while he read her various interesting passages from his latest book.

Where was the blasted woman, anyway? The bride and groom had departed two hours ago, and his other two daughters had arrived from preparing their sister, collected their husbands and left. It had been a long day and he was more than happy to have it done with.

He shifted in his chair, waiting for her arrival. Finally, the door opened and she entered. He immediately relaxed. "You know I can't concentrate on my book with you not here." He smiled at her and handed her a glass of sherry as was their practice.

She settled on her seat, took a tiny sip of sherry, and placed the glass on a small table in front of them. She laid her hands on her lap. Taking a deep breath, she said, "Henry, we must talk."

Sensing something disturbed her, he lowered his book and regarded her. "What is it, my dear?"

She raised her chin and stared him directly in his eyes. "Henry, I am presenting my resignation." She took out a sheet of vellum from her gown pocket and held it out toward him.

Henry studied her carefully, and set his glass down. "What are you talking about?"

"My resignation, Henry. I am resigning my position. I must leave."

"Selina, it has been a difficult couple of weeks. We are both tired. I don't wish to play games. Of course, you cannot resign."

She stood and paced. "Of course, I cannot *not* resign."

Finally realizing she was serious he stood and placed his hands on her shoulders. "What is the matter, Selina?"

She burst into tears and he wrapped his arms around her and laid her cheek against him. She sobbed on his chest for a bit, then he handed her a handkerchief. She looked up at him with a red nose, swollen eyes and took a deep, shuddering breath. "My work here is finished."

"I can see you are very upset, so I won't make light of your concerns, but you cannot leave."

"I was hired as a chaperone and companion to your daughters. Not that I've done such a wonderful job since they were all in a family way when they married."

Henry leaned back. "Marigold, too?"

"Yes," she sniffed. "You see, I wasn't even *good* at the job."

He pushed back the hair that had fallen from her hairdo onto her shoulder. "You have done the most remarkable job ever."

"How is that, Henry?"

"You've made me realize my life could continue after my dear departed wife left us." He made the sign of the cross, even though he wasn't Catholic. He took her hands and kissed each knuckle. "You made me believe in love again, Selina. And—"

She tightened her lips and closed her eyes. "Don't say it Henry."

He cupped her face, stroking her soft cheeks with his thumbs. "Marry me, my love."

With tear-filled eyes, she slowly shook her head. "No. I've told you before, Henry. I cannot marry you."

The End

Did you like this story? Please consider leaving a review on either Goodreads or the place where you bought it. Long or short, your review will help other readers discover new authors and make purchasing decisions!

Yes, Lord Pomeroy's story is next and *For the Love of the Lady* is now available:

Lord Henry Pomeroy's three daughters are finally married and happily settled in their own homes. He's looking forward to grandbabies and the company of Lady Crampton, the woman who acted as chaperone and companion to his daughters the past four years—and stole his heart in the meantime. Except she is moving out of his house!

Lady Selina Crampton has fallen hopelessly in love with her employer. Now that his youngest daughter is married, there is no longer a reason for her to remain since her work has come to an end.

Marriage is not possible, and the time has come to confront her demons and tell him why she has refused his numerous offers of marriage. It appears everyone is going to have their happy ending except them

For the Love of the Lady is available at various retailers: http://calliehutton.com/book/for-the-love-of-the-lady/

For the special treat I promised you,
Go to https://www.subscribepage.com/f3b6d8_copy

to receive a free copy of
A Little Bit of Romance, three short stories of lovers
reunited.
Enjoy!

ABOUT THE AUTHOR

Callie Hutton, the *USA Today* bestselling author of *The Elusive Wife*, writes both Western Historical and Regency romance, with "historic elements and sensory details" (*The Romance Reviews*). She also pens an occasional contemporary or two. Callie lives in Oklahoma with several rescue dogs and her top cheerleader husband of many years. Her family also includes her daughter, son, daughter-in-law and twin grandsons affectionately known as "The Twinadoes."

Callie loves to hear from readers. Contact her directly at calliehutton11@gmail.com or find her online at www.calliehutton.com. Sign up for her newsletter to receive information on new releases, appearances, contests and exclusive subscriber content. Visit her on Facebook, Twitter and Goodreads.

Callie Hutton has written more than 25 books. For a complete listing, go to www.calliehutton.com/books

Praise for books by Callie Hutton

A Wife by Christmas

"*A Wife by Christmas* is the reason why we read romance...the perfect story for any season." –The Romance Reviews Top Pick

The Elusive Wife

"I loved this book and you will too. Jason is a hottie

& Oliva is the kind of woman we'd all want as a friend. Read it!" --Cocktails and Books

"In my experience I've had a few hits but more misses with historical romance so I was really pleasantly surprised to be hooked from the start by obviously good writing." –Book Chick City

"The historic elements and sensory details of each scene make the story come to life, and certainly helps immerse the reader in the world that Olivia and Jason share." –The Romance Reviews

"You will not want to miss *The Elusive Wife*." –My Book Addiction

"...it was a well written plot and the characters were likeable." –Night Owl Reviews

A Run for Love

"An exciting, heart-warming Western love story!" – *NY Times* bestselling author Georgina Gentry

"I loved this book!!! I read the BEST historical romance last night...It's called *A Run For Love*." –*NY Times* bestselling author Sharon Sala

"This is my first Callie Hutton story, but it certainly won't be my last." –The Romance Reviews

A Prescription for Love

"There was love, romance, angst, some darkness,

laughter, hope and despair." –RomCon

"I laughed out loud at some of the dialogue and situations. I think you will enjoy this story by Callie Hutton." –Night Owl Reviews

An Angel in the Mail

"…a warm fuzzy sensuous read. I didn't put it down until I was done." –Sizzling Hot Reviews

Visit www.calliehutton.com for more information.

33752040R00100

Made in the USA
Lexington, KY
14 March 2019